Nos 1 & 2 (32 PAGES)   (COPYRIGHT)   PRICE-ONE PENNY.

THE KNIGHTRIDERS

By
THE AUTHOR OF
PAUL'S PERILS

E. & H. BENNETT, BEDFORD HOUSE, MAIDEN LANE, STRAND, LONDON.

THE KNIGHTRIDERS.

TOM BRERETON APPEALS FOR MERCY.

CHAPTER I.

HAMPSTEAD HEATH A HUNDRED YEARS AGO
—THE SHADOW OF THE GIBBET—A SON'S
VENGEANCE FOR HIS FATHER'S WRONGS.

ONE blustering night in January, a hundred
years ago, there stood upon one of the wildest
and most unfrequented parts of Hampstead
Heath, a gibbet—a ghastly token of the extreme power of a criminal code which seems
to us, in these days, to have been characterized
by unnecessary severity and ferocity.

Dependent from this gibbet hung all that
remained of a man, who in his life had borne
the name of Matthew Foster. He had been
put upon his trial on the charge of having
murdered the steward of Sir Lionel Faversham, in the shrubbery, near Faversham
House. He had been found guilty, was condemned, executed, and his body hung in

chains upon a gibbet near the scene of his crime; for from the spot where the corpse of the malefactor swung, creaking and rattling in the bitter blast, the chimneys and white facings of Faversham House could just be caught sight of peeping above the tops of a plantation of firs and chestnuts, about a quarter-of-a-mile away.

The felon's remains had hung in this horrible situation since the beginning of the previous September, and the autumnal rains had bleached face, hands, and clothing until they presented a uniform ghastly, gray, misty tint. The same rains had rusted the irons to a gloomy red, which contrasted strangely with the hideous spectacle which they encircled in their cold embrace.

Ever and anon, as the south wind swept across the heath, the body would give a lurch, and then the hook supporting it would creak with harsh dissonance against the ring above, startling the bewildered birds which, by the violence of the storm, had been driven from their nests in the neighbouring tree-tops.

Suddenly there came a gust of wind, so strong and overpowering that, like an unseen hand, it swung the body almost horizontally from the gibbet. The irons rattled, the hook shrieked dismally against the ring, and this time the grating sound of iron against iron was answered by a human voice, which, with a wail of agony, took up the sound and prolonged it into a scream.

Two figures then emerged from a little clump of trees, and with trembling steps drew near to the foot of the gibbet. They were a girl and a young man—the former being by two years the senior of the latter, although both were still in the very spring-time of youth.

With a shudder and a moaning cry, which might signify either pain or terror, the girl clung to her companion, and exclaimed:

"Are you sure you saw it, Claude?"

"Saw it, May? Yes; I saw it as plainly as —as—I now see yonder moon through that rift in the clouds. It was the figure of our poor father, just as he looked at that time, when you and I woke up at night and found him at our bedside. He had just come back from Holland, and we kissed him. Do you remember it, May?"

"Oh, yes, yes! But you know that our father is now—now—no more, so how could you see him? Let us return home! Surely you know—where—where this path will take us?"

"I do. But it was in this direction that the figure pointed, and then, for the first time, I felt that I must go and look upon a sight that—that—will perhaps break both our hearts. Listen! I was lying wide awake— I am sure I was quite wide awake, listening to the wind. I was not thinking of—of—of him who has gone, but of how we were to live to-morrow, when he came to my bedside."

"And you screamed?"

"No—no! I knew it was the apparition of our dear father. He looked at me so sor-

rowfully and so kindly that my eyes filled with tears. Then I saw the figure move towards the little window that looks this way, and it pointed in this direction. Then I sobbed out, 'father, father'; but it seemed to fade away like a mist, and I could hear nothing but the wind moaning round our cottage."

"It was very dreadful, Claude."

"Yes—yes; and yet I was more sad than frightened. So I rose, and called to you, May, to tell you that I was going out upon the heath, and you insisted upon coming with me. I have brought the old pistol with me. I know how to use it, and you need have no fear. We will to-night, for the first time, look upon that which we knew was to be seen upon the heath, and have never dared to approach, for I think that was what my father meant to-night."

While this brief conversation was in progress, the orphans—for such they were—had been ascending a raised portion of the heath, and when they reached the summit of what might be termed a little knoll, the young moon peeped out again from among the drifting clouds, and the girl, in the distance—a distance that, in the uncertain light, seemed much greater than it really was—caught sight of the gibbet.

With a cry of agony she threw herself upon her brother's breast, exclaiming in thrilling accents:

"Claude, Claude! it will break our hearts. It will—it will!"

Her companion guessed what it was that she had seen, and he shook with emotion.

It was some moments before he himself dared to look in the direction which May indicated.

At length, however, while her fair face was hidden on his breast, and her long silken hair streamed about him, he shaded his eyes with his disengaged hand, and looked towards the gibbet.

He could only just discern it, but the very shadow of it would have been enough to move him deeply. The moon once more disappeared behind a drifting cloud, and then, like a phantom, the gibbet was gone.

"May—dear May!" he whispered, "look up, and speak to me! I am quite sure that, awful as this thing is to us, the mere dread of how awful it must be is worse than the reality itself. Come on. Lean upon me as heavily as you please, I am sure that our dear father—who we know is in heaven—meant us to pay this sad visit to him to-night, as we were about to leave this neighbourhood to-morrow. Come on. Do not tremble so. Courage, May—courage! We are not so utterly wretched even now—poor, friendless, and forlorn as we really are—as he (Sir Lionel Faversham) who persecuted our poor father to death, and yet all the while had certain knowledge of his innocence!"

"He—he was innocent, Claude?"

"He was. He told us that he was innocent, and we will believe him, as we believe in Heaven."

"Oh, yes—yes! It is something to know he was not guilty of the crime they charged him with—that, although he perished so fearfully, he perished innocently! I dare not look up again, but—but I will not leave you! I will accompany you, but you must not ask me to look up again. Tell me you will not, for I know it would kill me to do so—or drive me mad, which would be worse. Oh, Claude—Claude! what is to become of us?"

She sobbed hysterically upon her brother's shoulder, and, stout-hearted as he was, he shook with emotion, and could not control his voice sufficiently to speak.

At length, however, by a great effort, he succeeded in uttering a few words of comfort to poor May.

"Creep gently on," he said, "and you shall not look up, if you do not wish to do so. For myself I feel that before I leave this place—I hope for ever—I ought to take one farewell glance at the remains of our poor father. Come on gently! See, the moon is peeping out again!"

It was so. Through a wide straggling opening in the clouds, the bright and beautiful new moon showed her slender crescent, and sent down a flood of silvery radiance upon the earth.

The two hapless mourners, for such in good truth they were, slowly approached the gibbet, and now they were so near to that dreaded and appalling object, that May felt she dared not raise her eyes from the ground lest they should be blasted by the awful sight before her.

To Claude it was evidently an act of desperate resolution to look up, and when at last he did so, it seemed almost as if, by some more than natural power, he had wrenched his head in that direction.

Immediately on the other side of the gibbet was a bridle path, and beyond that again was a deep declivity descending into the roadway for carriages, but all in that direction was gloom, for the tall fir trees completely prevented any observations beyond the gibbet, at which Claude continued gazing, until his eyes were so filled with tears that he could see nothing, and then he dashed them away with his disengaged hand, and looked again.

"Father, father," he said, "they murdered you. You did no murder, although Sir Lionel took an oath to say he saw you do it, and why was he so wicked, Heaven only knows."

"Claude, Claude," gasped May. "I—I never told you—but now, in the presence of this dreadful object, I feel that I ought."

"What do you mean, May?"

"I have thought at times that I knew why our poor father offended Sir Lionel Faversham; I do not rightly understand it, but Sir Lionel met me once upon the heath. He dismounted from his horse, and flinging the bridle across his arm, he insisted upon walking by my side to our cottage-door, and, as we went, he asked me if I should like a coach to ride in, and to be a lady. Then when we reached the cottage, he whispered something

to our poor father, who, thereupon, raised his hand and struck him. Sir Lionel left the cottage without a word, and our father turning to me, kissed my cheek, and said, 'Never mention this affair, my May. It is quite over.'"

"And soon after came the—the charge against our father of murdering the steward of Sir Lionel in the shrubbery of Faversham House," cried Claude. "Oh, Heaven! I see it all."

He clasped his hands, and dropped upon his knees at the foot of the gibbet.

"I swear," he cried. "I solemnly swear——"

"Oh, no, no," sobbed and entreated May. "Take no wild oath of revenge, Claude. Let us now pursue our original intention of going to London, and there seeking some honest means of livelihood, turning our backs for ever upon this place, which must, even to think of, be a horror to us."

"I will have revenge. No, not revenge, but justice. Henceforth, a sense of my father's wrongs will make me a foe to all mankind, except those who shall assist me to avenge them. Here, in presence of his poor remains, I swear——"

"Hush! hush! Claude, do you hear nothing?"

The tramp of a horse's feet upon the bridle path, just beyond the gibbet, came upon their ears, and, by one accord, they both leant forward to listen, in the direction whence the sound proceeded.

"Who is it?" whispered May. "Who is it?"

"Some chance traveller on the heath," replied Claude. "Listen! listen! and yet it is a strange time of night, and the road is seldom used except by those who are familiar with it, and who are going to Faversham House. Stand in the shadow, May—of—of——"

The gibbet he would have said, but with a shudder he paused, and did not pronounce the word.

May understood what he meant, and crouched down, sobbing by the foot of the appalling object.

The horseman evidently approached rapidly, and yet there seemed to be an unsteady, uncertain mode of progression about the steed, as it neared the spot where the corpse hung in its grim corselet of chains. It seemed as if the rider, by whip, rein, and spurs, were urging the animal to more speed than it chose, or had the power, from fatigue or otherwise, to make.

At length, just as another light cloud, which had produced a dimness over the surrounding scene, had swept across the face of the moon, and all was clear again, the horseman reached the point of his route, which was directly opposite to the gibbet; then it seemed as if some sudden panic had seized the horse, for it reared and plunged instead of proceeding onwards.

The moonbeams fell upon the figure of the traveller. The light wind carried his voice,

THE KNIGHTRIDERS.

as he uttered an imprecation, to the ears of Claude, who, clutching his sister's wrist with a violence that forced a slight scream from her lips, exclaimed :

"It is Sir Lionel !"

Like a lump of lead, and with a heavy, dashing sound, the dead body at this moment fell from the gibbet, and lay in a huddled-up ghastly mass at the feet of Claude—a mass of rusty iron, tattered clothing, and human remains.

Claude was upon his knees. Heavy drops of mortal agony rolled from his brow.

He plunged his hand into the breast of his clothing. The moonbeams fell glittering upon the barrel of a large holster pistol.

It was levelled across the dead body, finding a resting-place upon some of the ironwork that had enclosed the head of the gibbeted malefactor.

A sharp ringing report followed, and then horse and man rolled over the declivity, and disappeared in the profound darkness beyond.

There was a crashing of branches of trees— a struggle and a cry, followed by the thundering sound of the horse's hoofs, as he galloped madly onward, came upon the ears of Claude.

"'Tis done," he said. "'Tis done. The steed gallops home, but the rider remains upon the heath. 'Tis done! I could not miss such a shot as that. Father, you are avenged! You are avenged!"

CHAPTER II.

THE ROAD TO LONDON.

For a few moments now there was a death-like stillness, and, as more calm reflection came to his aid, Claude might well be alarmed at the consequences of the act he had just committed; for however, in the heat of his passion, or the excitement of the moment, it might bear the impress of a just retribution, its results could not be a matter of indifference.

It was from the clear intelligence and candid mind of his sister that Claude now sought for counsel what he was to do.

"May—May!" he said. "You know what has happened. May, speak to me—speak! Do not chill my heart by this silence. Dear May, speak to me!"

She was silent still, and then Claude, by a more accurate look at her pale face, discovered that she had fainted, and probably was quite unconscious of the act he had committed, and this thought produced a sudden revulsion of feeling in Claude.

"She knows nothing," he said to himself. "She fainted perhaps before the shot was fired, and it was not altogether fright which caused her to do so—exhaustion—weakness from want of proper food—has some share in it. Alas! that it should be so. That one so good and so beautiful as you are, my poor May, should want what to so many are superfluities. What can I do? What—what ought I to do?"

He rested his head upon his hands for some few moments, and then he made a resolution which will be best understood in its results, which were immediate.

After satisfying himself that May was still perfectly insensible, he gently crept from her side, and, passing the gibbet, made his way to the brink of the declivity down which Sir Lionel Faversham had rolled.

Then, holding tightly to an elder-tree which grew close to the edge of it, he tried to pierce with his eyes the gloom below, but he could see nothing. The rank vegetation effectually excluded all light, and, to all appearance, it seemed like looking into a well.

His determination, however, was made, and clutching at whatever roots or branches afforded him a chance of support, he slowly, but safely, descended the precipitous bank.

The depth was about thirty feet, and it took Claude some time before he reached the roadway that wound through the hollow of the heath at its base.

The moon was still struggling with the fleecy clouds, which seemed resolved, like some advancing host, to obliterate her brightness ; but at intervals there was light enough to distinguish one object from another.

The horse Claude knew was not there, but the rider he fully expected to find, nor was he disappointed, for a long, dark object met his gaze, and he thought for a long, that a strange groaning sound came faintly upon his ears.

Creeping along, with his body bent almost to the earth, and his hands outstretched, he made his way for the few paces that separated him from the body, and then he touched it.

At the moment of doing so he shuddered, for there was to his imagination something terrible about a corpse ; but, muttering some indistinct words to himself, in which the name of his sister was intermingled, he gathered courage, and began to execute his purpose, which was to find if the fallen man had money with him, which would enable him (Claude) and his sister to reach the metropolis in safety, and there subsist for a time until some better fortune should enable them to look more smilingly upon their fate.

"It is a just retribution," said Claude. "I —wonder if he carries a purse with him? This need never be known to May. It never shall be known, or to her perception each coin, and each particle of food purchased with it, would seem to be accursed."

His fingers trembled so, that it was only with the greatest difficulty that he could make the requisite search for the valuables which Sir Lionel might be supposed to have about him, but at length he found a long silken purse, which, from its weight, and the rich jingle of its contents, he judged contained what to him was a considerable sum in gold.

Twice his hands had touched a bunch of gold seals that hung from the watch pocket of Sir Lionel, and as often had Claude shaken his head, and left them, but now he lingered and listened attentively.

Not a sound came upon the night air, and

for the first time he showed a symptom of that mad-brained recklessness, which was a characteristic of his after career; for, snatching the watch from the pocket, where it had lain so snugly, he said:

"It's just as well to be able to know the time when one pleases."

The watch was a repeater, and in his haste, Claude pressed the spring, when, to his surprise, for he had no notion of such a contrivance, the little silvery bell struck one, and then chimed a quarter.

"Hush! hush!" said Claude, quite involuntarily, as he sprang to his feet.

He then placed both watch and money in his pocket, and commenced clambering again up the steep ascent to where he had left May.

There was a strange feeling at his heart now, and a kind of dizziness about his brain, which he could not, or fancied he could not, account for, although had he been a little more inquisitive into the sources of his feelings, and a little more candid with himself, he might have come to the conclusion that those feelings were the result of the consciousness that he was both a murderer and a robber. The excitement of a moment and strongly outraged feelings might be something in extenuation of the pistol-shot, but as regarded the purse and the watch, there could be invented no such excuses.

But the deed was done, so Claude scrambled upwards, and when he had just reached the brink of the precipice, he nearly fell the whole distance back again, so startled was he by the sudden touch of someone on his arm from above, and the pronunciation of his name.

The accents were those of May, and he recovered, saying:

"Oh, May, how you frightened me."

"Claude, Claude, what has happened? Tell me what has happened. Did not Sir Lionel fall over the bank?"

"Yes, and after that I heard the horse's hoofs upon the road to the 'Bull and Bush.'"

"Then he was not killed by his fall?"

"Certainly not."

"She knows nothing, and in her confusion has forgotten the pistol-shot," thought Claude, "and so far things turn out as I would wish them."

"Shall we go home?" said May, placing her arm across her eyes, lest they should take in a view of the horrible gibbet.

Claude was silent for a few moments, and then he said:

"You know, May, we have talked often of leaving here for ever. Why should we not do so to-night? There is nothing in the cottage that we need care for. Suppose we go to London at once, May, and see what fortune has in store for us. I have a little money, and we will so husband it, that it shall last us for a long time. What say you, May? The distance is short.—What is that?"

The jingle of bells and the creaking of wheels had come upon his ears, and almost as he asked the question of what it was, he replied to it, by adding:

"Oh, it is the Hendon waggon, which has just left the 'Bull and Bush.' There is a chance for us, May. We can meet it about half-a-mile further on, where the road rises to the level of the heath, and so go on to London, and never again with my good will shall I look upon Hampstead Heath."

"We are all alone," sobbed May, "in the wide world. We have no friends but each other. Where you go, Claude, there will I go, and Heaven knows, this place is too full of heart-breaking recollections to bind us to it. Let us go at once."

Claude was well pleased to find no opposition from May to leaving, and without casting another look at the awful spectacle that was at the foot of the gibbet, although they both lingered a little, and May wept bitterly, they left the spot, making their way across the heath, guided by the monotonous sound of the bells that were at the heads of the waggon horses.

"Stop!" cried Claude, as he and May met the waggon near the Castle. "Stop. Can you give us a lift to London? We can pay."

The waggoner paused, and stopped his team, and seemed to be considering a little, after which he said, half aloud:

"It's not very likely, now, surely, and I may as well earn a shilling."

Then he cried, in a louder voice:

"Scramble in at the back, you will find lots of straw. Be quick about it, for I am rather late to-night. That's right. But, look you, if your places are wanted, you must get out again, and ask no questions; mind that now."

"There will be room enough for us, and a dozen others too, I should think," said Claude, as he assisted May into the waggon, and sprang in after her.

"I don't know that," muttered the waggoner, "and I am half afraid now of the Captain. Yet it's a chance, and I don't see why I should not earn an extra shilling when I can. They are only a boy and girl, too, and can be easily put out if needs be; and yet—I don't know—I wish I hadn't——"

Thus muttering his doubts and fears about something which was quite unintelligible to Claude, the waggoner put his horses again in motion, and they crept at a lazy pace over the heath, which then had none of the snug villas and smart cottages about it that it has now; for, with the exception of two trees, and Lord Mansfield's large house, there was not a more desolate spot to be found at night than the beautiful heath of Hampstead.

For a good half-mile further on no house or light was to be found, and the waggon, which was a large covered one, with an amazing width of entrance at the back, and containing nothing but a quantity of loose straw, had advanced about half that distance, when Claude's heart beat violently as he heard distinctly the gallop of a horse across the heath, for a dread that in some inexplicable way the murder and robbery of Sir Lionel Faversham might have been discovered, and suspicion placed upon him, was busy in his brain.

A sensation of absolute sickness came over him, as he heard the hollow ringing sound of the horse's hoofs on the common.

The waggon stopped.

"Hilloa!" cried the waggoner, "do you hear, or have you gone to sleep? You can't stay any longer. Come out directly, or it will be the worse for you! Come out, I say, or we shall all be in a nice mess. Confound me for a fool, to take you till I was clear of the common!"

"Who is it—who is it?" cried Claude, as the sound of the horse's feet came nearer and more distinct, giving evidence that he who was approaching would soon be close to the waggon.

"You would be none the wiser if I told you," replied the man, speaking hurriedly, and betraying the utmost anxiety to get rid of his guests. "Scramble out—any way, so that you be off at once!—It's too late—he's here, and I'm in for it at last."

All this happened with such rapidity, and May clung so closely to her brother, who was likewise rather entangled in the straw that lay so thickly at the bottom of the waggon, that, even had he felt fully inclined to obey the hurried and rather vehement commands of the waggoner, he could not have done so with sufficient celerity to save the latter part of his speech, to the effect that it was too late.

Under these circumstances, then, Claude did the best thing he could, which was to remain ready to act according to circumstances, getting as far as he could, with May still clinging to him, towards the upper end of the capacious vehicle.

The night was now darker than before, for a mass of clouds had come across the young moon, threatening to obscure its light effectually for some hours, so that Claude had no sense but that of hearing, through which he could obtain any information.

"What do you tell me, old Peter?" cried a careless, laughing sort of voice. "Two persons in the crib—eh? A girl and a boy! Well, well—no matter. I like good company, and they will be none the worse for a ride to London with me. Where are they? Tell them to get up to the far end, and they will come to no harm. Throw open the canvas, Peter—don't you hear that there are half-a-dozen horsemen on my track?"

To the intense astonishment of Claude, and the alarm of May, the horse, with its rider, bounded lightly into the waggon, and the canvas at the back was immediately closed upon them both.

"Down, 'Silversides'—down, mare!" cried the man, and, by the motions of the horse among the straw, Claude was aware that it had lain down on its side.

He drew May as far as possible away from dangerous contiguity to the animal's feet, and then, mustering courage to speak, he said:

"Sir, we are not disposed to be in your way. We only want a lift to London."

"Very good," was the careless reply; "but, mark me, my lad, if you prate of what you have seen to-night, I'll find you out, if you were as difficult to get at as truth in the bottom of a well, and then it will be the worse for you. Who are you?"

"My name is Claude——"

"Hush!" said May.

He removed, somewhat impatiently, the little hand which she had placed upon his lips to ensure his silence, and, after a slight hesitation, added:

"Duval, and this is my sister, May. Pray, who are you?"

"Humph!—you want to know who I am?"

"I should like to know, for, somehow, I think we shall be friends yet."

"Do you, my lad? Well, then, I don't recollect my real name, but, among my pals, I am called Sixteen-string Jack, and this is my mare, 'Silversides.'"

CHAPTER III.

SIXTEEN-STRING JACK—THE BROTHER AND SISTER SEPARATE.

AFTER the mysterious personage, who had so unceremoniously sprung with his horse into the waggon, had thus spoken, there was a pause of some few minutes duration, for neither Claude nor his sister could make much of the rather singular name of Sixteen-string Jack, and they feared to comment upon it, lest they might offend one who, evidently, had the power to turn them out of the waggon if he chose.

"What are you thinking about?" at length cried Jack. "I warrant, now, you are nicely puzzled to know what I am, so I will tell you. I keep a toll on the Great North Road, and, as I don't like to trust anybody to collect my dues, I do it myself; and, as there are unreasonable people, who object to pay, I carry a good brace of bull-dogs with me."

"Bull-dogs, sir?" said Claude.

"Ay—pistols. These are my bull-dogs, and they never bark when I don't want them; but when I do, they open tongue to some purpose. Then, again, some folks, after they have paid, go prating about it, and get others to ask disagreeable questions, so that I give the spur to my good steed, 'Silversides,' and off we are over hill and dale, like the wind. It's a brave life, and I'm the real lord of many manors—the king of the road—and whoever travels by moonlight is a subject of mine, and must pay my taxes. What do you think of all that, my lad?"

"I hardly know what to think," said Claude.

"Don't speak to him," whispered May—"don't speak to him—he's a highwayman, Claude. Let us get out of here, and walk."

"Hist!" cried Sixteen-string Jack, suddenly. "Not a word, on your lives. Don't you hear?"

Claude listened, and distinctly heard the tramp of horses' feet; and, in a few moments, a loud, authoritative voice cried:

"Hilloa! Pull up, waggoner. How far have you come, my man?"

And, by the trampling of horses and the bustle around, Claude felt certain that several horsemen had congregated about the waggon.

He could hear, too, by the hard breathing of the steeds, that they had been going at a quick pace, while the tone of inquiry of him who spoke was hurried and anxious.

"Woa!" cried the waggoner, and the horses paused, while the jingling of the bells at their heads nearly ceased. "Woa! Anan, sir? What *wur yow* a saying?"

"How far have you come down the road, my man?"

"Oh, how far? From Goulder's Green."

"Has a horseman passed you on the heath?"

"One did—a chap on a bay horse; and wasn't he a-going it—hares and hounds! I thought he'd a been right over me, waggon and all—I did. 'Hark ye, my man,' says he, 'if you say you saw anyone to-night on the heath,' says he, 'you may as well cut your own throat,' says he, ''cos it will save me the trouble,' says he, 'of finding you out, and cutting it for you,' says he; and then off he was like a shot. Drat him! I ain't afeared of him—drat his impudence!"

"Our man, without a doubt," said the horseman. "Which way did he go?"

"Beyant there—to Caen Wood, I take it."

"Follow me, gentlemen. This will be a good night's work if we rid the neighbourhood of that notorious highwayman, Sixteenstring Jack. I fired at him, and perhaps he is wounded, in which case he cannot hold out long. This way, gentlemen. Follow me, and don't spare whip or spur."

The party of pursuers galloped off across the heath, and the waggoner, without taking any further notice of the transaction, put his horses into motion again, and entered the village of Hampstead.

"They were looking for you," said Claude to the highwayman.

"They were, my lad; but, you see, they are baulked. I wonder what the time is. I gave my watch this morning to Nat Eyles, and the one a gentleman lent me about half-an-hour since, upon the heath, has run down."

"I can tell you the time," said Claude, on the impulse of the moment, producing the repeater he had taken from the pocket of Sir Lionel Faversham. "I can tell you exactly the time, I dare say, and it strikes, too, though I don't quite know how to make it."

It was too dark for the watch to be seen, but the highwayman was surprised to find that such an article was in the possession of such a lad, and he said:

"Hand it to me. If it be a repeater I can make it strike."

By the feel, rather than by any aid from the dim light that now and then, from a miserable oil-lamp, came into the waggon, Claude managed to place the watch in the hands of his new acquaintance, and then he had the pleasure, in a moment, of hearing the little fairy-like bell sound the hour.

The different persons in that waggon were very differently affected by those slight and musical sounds.

The highwayman felt that there was a mystery attached, and he held his peace, and listened for the remarks of his companions, as being most likely to afford him some clue to what was as yet a perfect puzzle.

Claude was occupied with a mixed feeling of joy and pain. He listened to the sounds of the repeater with almost childish pleasure, but he felt at the same moment that May's suspicions would be aroused, and that he must in some way or other, either by falsehood, which he held in contempt, or by the plain truth, satisfy his sister's doubts.

But to poor May the tinkling sounds were full of naught but horror.

Almost intuitively she seemed to be aware that the trinket was the prize of some lawless deed, committed when or how she knew not.

She had penetrated enough of their fellow companion's character to dread any closer connection with him, and her soul was overshadowed by dread of disasters none the less appalling for being undefined, which loomed fearfully out from the darkness of the future.

She felt that her brother's fate was in some way connected with the possession of the watch, which had appeared among them as mysteriously as if it were indeed one of those gifts of seeming value with which the spirits of evil were said to tempt men's souls.

A moment only elapsed, when, in a startled and fearful voice, she broke the silence.

"Oh, Claude, Claude," she sobbed, "how came you by a watch?"

"What matters it," answered Claude, "where it came from? I have it, and that ought to be sufficient. It will make a pretty ornament for you, dear May, at holiday times, when fortune smiles once more upon us."

"Nay, talk not so, dear brother," whispered May, "I could feel no pleasure in wearing it, unless I knew how you came by it, and poor orphans as we are, and homeless wanderers, too, Claude, I dare not hope for happy times for many a weary day to come. Set my heart at ease, then, and do not aggravate our present misfortunes by filling my mind with fears that I dare not give utterance to;" and May threw herself weeping on his neck.

"Fears! what have you to fear, May? Did you never hear of one person losing a watch on a dark night, and another person finding it?"

"Such a thing is quite possible," said May, "but even then, Claude, the watch would not be yours to keep or give to me. It would be your duty to hand it over to those who would find an owner for it."

"And many thanks I should get for that, sister. No, no, dry your tears, dear May, and rest satisfied that the watch shall not pass from my hands to another, owner or not owner, unless he who demands it is a better man than myself."

"Claude, Claude," exclaimed poor May,

"how can you grieve me by saying so; you cannot mean what you say."

"Ho, ho," cried Sixteen-string Jack, "I find you are a lad of mettle—eh? Come, you may trust me, my lad. How came you by it? It's a dangerous companion for you, if there should be any hue and cry. You might do a worse thing than make me your friend in such an affair. You are silent—you are afraid to trust me. Perhaps that's natural; but have not I trusted you? A word from you to the horsemen that a minute since stopped the waggon, and I should have been taken. I could not have held my own against such odds, and then, as sure as to-morrow's sun will rise, I should have swung at Tyburn. I would fain do you a good turn. This watch may be your destruction."

"Keep it yourself, sir," said May, "and for Heaven's sake, Claude, say not another word about it."

"Nonsense, pretty face," laughed Jack; "for a pretty face I am sure you have; however, let him speak out."

"I took it," said Claude, "upon the heath, from Sir Lionel Faversham."

"You robbed Sir Lionel Faversham to-night upon the heath? The deuce you did! And is this the first little adventure of the sort?"

"The very first."

May burst into tears, and clung convulsively to her brother, as she sobbed:

"The last, likewise—the last; Claude, send back the watch, and ask for forgiveness. Oh, Claude, I thought we were unhappy, but I knew not what wretchedness really was until now; you will do as I implore you? Speak, speak to me, and say you will do so."

"A dangerous course, miss," said Jack; "it's too late."

"Yes," said Claude, drawing a long breath, "yes, it's too late."

May sobbed bitterly, while the highwayman whispered to Claude:

"You have done now what cannot be undone. As for expecting any mercy, even if you chose to seek it from Sir Lionel Faversham, you might as well expect a famished tiger merely to pass you in a lonely place with his compliments. If he can find you, he will not rest until you are in the cart on your road to Tyburn. You are fortunate in coming across me, for I can afford you both counsel and protection. When we get to London, I can find an asylum for yourself and your sister until the hue and cry is over, and then you can take your own course, and, unless I am very much mistaken, I can guess tolerably well what that course will be. A good horse!—a pair of pistols!—a light heart!—and——"

"The road!" cried Claude. "Life on the road! I am poor and friendless—my father's bones bleach upon the heath. The sense of deep wrongs lies rankling at my heart, and I cannot bow and smile my way through life for a sup or a crust. The road for me! A short life and a merry one, and the sooner it begins the better."

"Hurrah!" said Jack; "you are the lad for me. Here we are at the 'King's Head,' near Kentish Town, where I can give you a welcome until to-morrow, and then take you to a safer place still."

"No, no," cried May, in a voice that was almost a shriek of despair. "No, no—Claude, you are mad!—you know not what you say! I implore you by the tie that binds us, orphans as we are, to each other, to pause. For my sake, if not for your own, I beseech you not to give way to this frightful temptation. If you would seek happiness or peace, seek it in honour, truthfulness, and in honesty. You are on the threshold yet of life; you have not sinned deeply. Oh, plunge not rashly onwards in the desperate course you suggest."

"Really, my dear," said the highwayman in a bantering tone, "you——"

"Peace, sir," said May, "interrupt me not, "I am talking with a sister's love to a brother. Shame, shame, upon you who have become hardened in vice, to strive to warp him round to a love of your own evil courses. Shame, shame, upon you, for your own guilt, but doubly shameful is it to snatch from a right course a being who cannot know, as you know, the evil that presents itself to him in such fleeting but alluring colours."

"Very good," said Jack, "say your say, my lass, and let your brother take his own course, it doesn't matter to me; my career is fixed."

The waggon had stopped, and a glare of light came into its interior from a lantern that a man who had come out of a public-house door held up, while he shaded his eyes with his hands.

The scene within the waggon was a strange one.

The highwayman's horse, which occupied by far the greater portion of the interior, lay upon its side, while Sixteen-string Jack kept his hand upon the creature's head.

The highwayman's dress could now be distinguished—he wore a scarlet coat with large lapels, slightly disclosing an embroidered waistcoat, and the lace ends of a rich, but not by any means scrupulously clean, cravat. From the tops of his boots hung a knot of coloured ribbon, from which he derived his cognomen of Sixteen-string Jack, and take him altogether, he looked the very *beau ideal* of a knight of the road at that strange period, when highwaymen were as much public characters as Members of Parliament are now.

Claude was standing up, and steadying himself by holding part of the awning of the waggon, while May was kneeling at his feet in an attitude of entreaty that she had assumed to warn him from his desperate purpose of taking to the road for a livelihood.

"Hilloa, Captain!" said the man; "what's it all about? Have you got some company?"

"I have," replied the highwayman, and then, turning to May, he added, "You are doing me a great injustice; you fancy I want to persuade your brother to go upon the road, but you quite forget that he has been there already, and that all I offer him is protection from the consequences of what has happened on Hampstead Heath to-night. Do you fancy now that he has nothing else to do but to wish to lead a quiet, virtuous life, and that he will be permitted to do so? I can tell you it is not so. He will be hunted down for what he has already done, and all I want him to do, is to stand at bay a little. But you may settle it between you, what can it matter to me?"

"Claude, do not answer him; Claude—Claude!"

She rose, and flung herself on her brother's neck, so that he was prevented from making any movement towards Sixteen-string Jack, but he held out his hand, and the highwayman nodded, as much as to say, "I comprehend you—you have made your choice;" and then, pointing to the inn, the door of which was kept rather uncomfortably open, he paused for a moment, as if expecting Claude to make an effort to release himself from his sister's detaining embrace, and follow him.

"May," whispered Claude, "May, you know not what you advise, I will speak to you to-morrow; let us to-night accept of rest and shelter where we can."

"No, no. Better starve—better be destitute in the streets, than enter that house."

"I cannot make such a return for a kind offer."

"Say you will not, Claude, and I shall understand you, although I shall never believe that it is you who speak."

"Listen to me, May; you shall be kept like a lady, your happiness and comfort shall be my first care; you shall want for nothing. Let me go—let me go."

She clung tighter still to him; Sixteen-string Jack laughed, and Claude's cheek reddened, for he thought, as boys are apt to think, that it reflected upon his manhood to be detained thus by his sister, so he spoke more angrily.

"May, I say, release me!"

As these words were uttered he flung her from him, and jumped from the waggon.

With a cry of grief she followed him, and clung again to his apparel, but again he shook her off, and rather roughly, too, so that had not Sixteen-string Jack interposed his arm she would have fallen; but when she found to whom she owed the temporary support, she shrank back from him with a shudder, and clasping her hands, looked for a moment or two earnestly at Claude.

"Come, sister May," he said; "the rain is falling, and the wind blows still; come in."

"No," she said, "no; since it must be so, farewell, Claude."

In a moment she darted off, and was lost to sight in the darkness.

"Stop—stop," cried Claude; "May, you must not go alone and destitute. Stop—oh, stop!—listen, May, I have more to say to you."

He would have rushed after her, but the highwayman held him by the arm, as he cried:

"Pho! pho! she won't run far. You will have her back again soon. Where is she to go to? Make yourself comfortable. Landlord, bring a bowl of punch, and let it be the best you can make. I and my young friend must be better acquainted."

"But—but," said Claude, "but my sister——"

"Oh, you will see her again soon enough. Besides, what idea can you have of her affection if she starts off from you the first time there is any little difference of opinion, while you, as a man, ought to know best what to do?"

This was attacking Claude at his weak point.

"Oh, yes," he said. "We men are not to be guided by women."

"Of course not. Come in, come in. The punch, landlord, the punch. The wind is cold, indeed, to-night. Claude Duval, you will be famous; I am no bad judge of such matters, and something seems to tell me that there never was yet a knightrider who will be able to compare with you. I shall be proud of you as a friend. Come on, come on, and we will talk more of it."

CHAPTER IV.

THE LONELY HORSEMAN—THE NIGHT ATTACK —THE HUT—A FAMILY CARRIAGE.

Two years have elapsed since the incidents recorded in the previous chapters.

It is a cold—bitterly cold night in January. The east wind is scattering sleet and hail like small sparks of sharpened steel through the air, and all, as far as the eye can reach, is darkness and desolation.

In the midst of such a scene, and at such a time, a solitary horseman is trotting across Ealing Common.

It is not by a regular bridle road that this horseman proceeds; on the contrary, whenever by the sound—and it is only by the sound that he can come to an opinion, in consequence of the darkness around him—he finds that his horse is on a beaten track, he turns aside again until there is nothing beneath the cautious hoofs but the green turf, or small pools of water into which it almost each moment splashes.

"Now, by all that's good," muttered the horseman, as he clenched his teeth against the keen wind, and, with his disengaged right hand, dashed the half-blinding sleet from before his eyes, "I would not have come out on such a night as this, had it not been that the gaming-table has so completely cleared my purse that it sadly lacks replenishing. It will look positively ungentlemanly to stop anybody on such a night, but needs must when a certain old friend of mine drives, so, hurrah for my old luck, and here I am upon the high road at last."

There was just light enough to distinguish the principal road that went across the common from the darker colour of the grass that fringed it, and the solitary horseman now kept within half-a-dozen paces on the turf by the side of it.

By the turn he had now made at right angles to his former course, his back was turned towards the cutting sleet that was driving through the air, and he certainly got on much more comfortably than before, while he half sang to himself a popular air of the day, and when he fancied, and in most cases it was but fancy, he saw a hillock before him, he made the obedient horse give a demi-vault, which it executed with surprising grace and ease.

"Ah, my good Nell!" apostrophized the rider. "My good Nell, what should I do without thee? What should I be without thee, my gallant lass—fleet of foot—long in wind—sagacious, and more faithful than many human beings. I love thee, my Nell!"

As he uttered this panegyric upon his horse, he patted the neck of the animal, which, by a short neigh, seemed to be fully sensible that just then it was a special object of its master's commendations, and to be well pleased accordingly.

Suddenly the horseman gave the rein a peculiar touch, and his steed stood as motionless as though it had been carved in stone.

"Hush! hush!" he said; "my old acuteness of hearing is bothered by the wind and the sleet, or I hear the sound of horse's feet."

After then listening for a few moments he still was in doubt, for he suddenly flung himself lightly off the horse, and placed his ear nearly on a level with the ground to listen. This process quite satisfied him, and, vaulting into the saddle again, he said:

"Yes, someone comes. I am not mistaken, and I have only to hope that his purse is well lined. It will be a great insult to a gentleman of the road if it be not, and must be resented accordingly. We shall see. The horse's footsteps sound clean and clear, as though it was no common hack. Now Nell, my lass, we may have a little adventure to warm our bloods, and, faith, we need it on such a night as this."

The sound of an approaching horse at an easy canter was now plainly perceptible, and the highwayman, for such our readers, of course, conclude him to be, walked his steed gently along the road, to meet the advancing traveller, and the dusky figures of a horse and man were soon seen against the leaden-coloured sky.

Thus approaching each other, but a very few minutes could elapse ere the highwayman and his intended victim came face to face, and saw as much of each other as upon such a night could be seen.

"Halt!" said the highwayman; "halt! Answer me one question, Sir Traveller, and answer it upon your honour."

"What do you mean? Keep off, as you value your life," said the traveller, in stern accents; "I am armed."

"Very good. It is unsafe to travel unarmed, and not always safe even with arms; but to my question: Are you a gentleman? By which I mean, one who eats the bread of idleness, and is not engaged in any business pursuits."

"A gentleman!" said the stranger. "Who dare dispute my right to that title?"

"Good. I never condescend to stop any but gentlemen, and since you assert your right to the designation,—stand and deliver!"

"What?"

"Your money—watch—rings—or, your life!"

"Now, by Heavens, this is the most barefaced and impudent attempt at robbery I ever heard of. You will consult your own safety by getting from before my path."

"You are mistaken, sir; I wish to behave towards you with all due courtesy, but you will best consult your own ease by complying with my demand. As for my safety, I set my life upon casts like these, and am willing to stand the hazard of the die."

"Take it, then," said the stranger; and, drawing a pistol from his pocket, he snapped it in the face of the highwayman.

The powder flashed in the pan, without discharging the weapon, and the traveller, casting it to the ground with an imprecation, was fumbling in his pocket for another, which did not seem to be so ready to his hand, when, with a suddenness and a violence that could not be resisted, the highwayman closed with him, and grasping him by the collar, flung him from his seat.

"You should keep your powder dry!" he exclaimed.

"Villain," cried the traveller, as he lay half-stunned by the fall.

"Not so," replied the highwayman; "if I were, what would there be to hinder me repaying you in kind for your intention to blow my brains out, by actually performing that process upon the small quantity you evidently only possess. Once more, your money and valuables!"

He had dismounted; and while his horse, "Nell," stood profoundly still, the stranger's steed, alarmed at the confusion, scampered away over the common, and was out of sight in a moment in the darkness.

"Take my purse; and here, too, is my watch. I have but one ring, and that I wish to keep—not so much on account of its value, as from recollections connected with it."

"Oh, certainly. Don't say another word about it."

"You are chivalric in your way," added the gentleman, as he made a vain effort to rise, but found that he had struck his head so severely against a stone, that the darkness seemed full of strange grotesque shapes, swimming before him. "I—I ask you a favour——"

"What is it?"

"I can scarcely speak. I think I shall faint from this fall. There is a travelling carriage coming with ladies, and one man; spare them. One lady is an invalid."

"Which way is it coming? From town or

country. Nay, you have already said so much, you may as well give me full information. You are silent—eh? Why, he has fainted, I suppose. He must be seriously hurt, for it is not from any faint-heartedness he has gone off in this way. But if people will be obstinate, and resist the tolls, they must take the consequences. I won't leave him here though, to be run over by somebody. I can't be far off old Jarvis's place at Hanger Hill. If I could get him there, he would be safe until the morning, and Jarvis could easily say he found him lying on the common. It shall be so. 'Nell,' my lass, 'Nell!'"

The horse was close to him in a moment.

"This is not what you are exactly used to," continued the highwayman, "but, at a pinch, you won't object, I dare say. Humph! a tolerable weight, though thin enough."

He lifted the insensible form of the traveller, and laid it as well as he could across the horse's back, and then taking the bridle in his hand, he guided Nell across the common, with which, at that dark hour, he seemed wonderfully familiar, until he reached some trees skirting a low hedge, which formed the boundary of a little garden surrounding a miserable-looking cottage. Then he paused, and blew a whistle in a peculiar manner.

In a few moments a man appeared at the door of the cottage, with a lantern in his hand.

"Jarvis, it's I," cried the highwayman.

"My noble Captain, has anything happened amiss?"

"No, but here is a gentleman who has had a fall upon the common, and muddled his brains for a time. I want you to let him lie quiet till the morning, when no doubt he will be all right, and relieve you from further trouble. If he remains on the common, who knows but somebody might rob him—eh, Jarvis?"

The man put the lantern on the ground, and, by placing his hands on his sides, was evidently upon the point of bursting into a roar of laughter at what he considered a famous joke, when he was checked by the highwayman's crying:

"Peace, peace! I have no time to spare."

"Oh, certainly, Captain; another job coming, I suppose?"

"Possibly."

The still insensible stranger was lifted from the horse's back, and carried into the hut, after which the highwayman remounted his horse, and went back to the common at a hard gallop, until he reached the main road again, when once more he drew rein and listened.

"I hear nothing," he muttered. "Could he have been deceiving me for any purpose? I am quite certain no travelling carriage has passed here to-night. Shall I be content with what I have already done, or shall I wait for it? Humph! ladies, he said, and one man; there will be more purses than one, and who knows but this fellow may take credit to himself, when he returns to tell the story, for

frightening me from an attack on the carriage. No, my Nell, we will not be put off by the story of an invalid lady; and if there be one, we will be so gentle that she shall feel no shock to her nerves. Ha! It comes."

He distinctly heard, during a lull in the wind, the grinding sound of carriage wheels in the soft, sandy soil. The horse, too, pricked up its ears, and seemed fully alive to the excitement of its master's adventures.

He paced slowly onwards in the direction of the approaching sounds, while the highwayman, in a low, but not unmusical voice, sang to himself a fragment of a popular ditty.

Whenever the wind lulled a little he paused to listen, but it was only occasionally that he could hear anything, for as the wind was blowing from him towards the carriage all sounds were carried away from him.

Presently, however, he became quite certain that a vehicle was approaching, so he slackened his horse's pace, and turned him once more upon the grass that bordered the roadway, so that no sound of the animal's footsteps should create a premature alarm.

Shepherd's Bush was at that time a wild and desolate place, and the road from it to Southall was so celebrated for the daring deeds of highwaymen, that it was no uncommon thing for people to turn back instead of crossing Ealing Common if there happened to be the least suspicion that one of these night adventurers was upon it, and it was for this reason that Claude took such precautions to remain unheard.

And now, about a quarter-of-a-mile away from him, he saw two faint, star-like lights, which he recognized at once as carriage-lamps, so that he had a capital guide to the vehicle's approach, and was able to take up his station in that part of the road which he deemed best suited to his purpose.

There was a hollow of about fifty feet in length, and it was in the lowest part of it, where the highwayman reined in his steed. There was behind him a clump of fir-trees which effectually prevented his figure being seen against the background of night sky.

These trees, too, tempered the wind considerably, so that this spot where he had resolved to stop the carriage was the calmest upon the whole common, as well as, in consequence of its lying so low, the heaviest bit of road for the tired horses to struggle through; and therefore one where stopping them would be most easily achieved.

CHAPTER V.

THE HEIR-AT-LAW—BEAUTY IN TEARS—THE PROTECTOR.

THE travelling carriage which was doomed to be brought to an abrupt standstill on Ealing Common, had emblazoned upon its panels, the arms of one of the most ancient Oxfordshire families, and it contained personages so different in mind and manners, that even if it were not intimately connected with our story, it would be not a little curious to peep into it, and see how they behaved themselves individually towards each other.

It was one of those old-fashioned roomy family coaches that were so much approved of at the time of our story, and that held six people without the least inconvenience.

It was drawn by a pair of strong but lazy horses, who never condescended to go at a faster rate than a quiet jog-trot of about five miles an hour, which was thought very good work indeed, more especially as the roads were but indifferent. On this occasion, however, there was a light load, for only four persons occupied the interior of the carriage.

One of them was an elderly lady, who seemed absorbed in painful reflections, for every now and then she shook her head, and gave utterance to a deep sigh.

Then there was sitting next to her a young lady, who held the old lady by the hand, and who, in a whisper at intervals, said something to her, which was intended to be cheering.

On the opposite seat, crammed into one corner, was a younger lady, and all her efforts seemed to be to get as far as possible from a man who was on the seat beside her, and who was about one of the finest specimens of the "mashers" of the period that could probably have been found.

His coat was sky-blue, and had cloth enough about its skirts to make another one of the fashion now in vogue. His ruffles descended to the tips of his fingers. His hat diminished at the top to a ridiculously small circumference, and he held in both hands a riding-whip, with the silver end of which he patted his mouth with great complaisance.

"Well, cousin Cicely," he said, "you don't seem the worse for your journey as yet, at any rate, do you now?"

This speech was evidently intended to procure a reply from the young lady, who was holding the hand of her elder companion, but it failed in that object, for the only notice taken of it consisted in a slight—a very slight —inclination of the head from her.

"Well," he added, after another pause. "You may as well speak, I'm sure."

"What would you have her say?" inquired the old lady, tremulously. "You cannot expect that we should feel very happy."

"Hem! Well, I don't know that."

"What! Are we not now destitute?"

"Oh, no, no, I—that is you can look to me, you know. I used always to be counted a generous sort of fellow. The fact is, you take too much to heart the loss of the little property at Guildford; but it can't be helped, you know. You came into possession, all of you, because it was thought I was drowned on the river; but, Lor' bless you, I wasn't drowned at all. The fact is I was picked up when insensible by a Dutch smuggler, and carried to Holland, that I was. He! he! he! Well, you must know I had no money, and——"

"You have told us all this before," said the old lady.

"Well, I was only saying. He! he! he! Tom Brereton is like a cat, he always lights upon his legs—everybody says that. Well, you see, a fat little Dutch girl fell in love with me, so I borrowed some money of her, and gave her the slip. He! he! he! Then I came to England, and found my old governor dead; and as I was supposed to be drowned, you and your family had walked from a couple of attics in Bloomsbury, into the little Guildford property. Your son, too, must, to put himself forward in the army, borrow £100 on it. Lor', how you all stared when you saw me. Well, you ask me to come to London with you, to go to your friend Hammerston, the lawyer, and talk about it. Yes, says I— talk away. He! he! he! And here I am. This is my carriage, you know, properly speaking, though you do ride on the best seat."

"We will resign it to you," said the young girl.

"Oh, no, no—never mind me, I only just mentioned it, that's all."

"You may be the son of my poor brother, whom I call poor because he was uncharitable," said the old lady, "or you may not, for, as you know very well, if you be the person you represent yourself to be, I have not seen you since you were a child."

"If I be? Well, come, that is good. But the lawyer will soon put that to rights; and as for not seeing you and your family, the old governor who has gone to glory, I suppose, used to say, 'Tom, always keep out of the way of your poor relations. They will borrow your legs else, and leave you nothing but stumps to walk upon.' He! he! he! Good that was."

"And kind," said the younger girl, who sat on the same seat with him, and who now, in a tone of bitter sarcasm, pronounced these two words.

"Well, miss pert," said Tom Brereton, "I don't see that you have any right to meddle with it. You are only——"

"My friend," interrupted the young lady opposite, "and as such entitled to respect."

"Respect a fiddlestick! Upon my life, for people going out of their property, you are about as confounded a set of stuck-up folks as ever I heard of. I suppose your son, Markham, old lady, has got to London by this time, eh?"

"I don't know, sir," said the old lady.

"Oh, don't you, ma'am? Well, I can't say I see why you should all of you be in such a way. You were poor before, and you will only be poor again, you know. I daresay you thought it an uncommonly nice thing to drop into £750 a year; but, after all, you can go back to the two attics in Bloomsbury, you know, and try and get some sort of work to do, so as to pay me off by degrees what you have already spent of mine. He!—he!—he! I think I ought to have rent for the house, too, for as long as you have been in it—upon my life I do."

"Can it be possible?"

"Rather."

"Alas—alas! And this is the amount of mercy I am to expect from my brother's son. Young man, we have told you candidly that we are now going to call upon a lawyer, to ask him what you can demand, and what you cannot."

"Oh, I know that, but you need not all of you be in such a pet with me. If you had been civil, you need not have given yourself half the trouble. You were not over inclined to allow me even a seat in the coach, though I did ask for it. He!—he!—he!—my own coach, too. And why you should all be offended, just because I told Cicely she was pretty, and gave her the least tickle in the world, I don't know."

"If I were to inform my son, sir, of your conduct," said the old lady, "I would not answer for your safety one moment afterwards. I wish he had remained with us; but one reason why he did not was, that the road is so infested with highwaymen, that he thought it best to ride on till we were quite among the houses to clear the way."

"Highwaymen! Bless my heart, you don't think there's any danger, do you? I've got £20 in my pocket, besides all my papers to prove who I am. Bless me! I—I don't feel comfortable at the idea of a highwayman at all, somehow. I like my money."

"No doubt of it," said the girl on the seat with him.

"Of course I do, but I like my life better; and would rather, of course, like any reasonable man, pay something any day than be in any danger."

"So I should think."

"Ah, to be sure! You are, after all, a more sensible girl than I thought you. Now, I tell you what we will do if a highwayman should stop us. I'll just slip down among the straw, and you can all of you say there are no persons but women here, and beg them to let you go."

"I should rather be inclined," said Cicely, "to direct attention to you, as bearing the semblance of a man, in order to protect our riches."

"No—no! You wouldn't do that now. How uncommonly unfriendly. Where are we now, I wonder. Hoi—hoi! postilion, where are we now?"

"Ealing Common, sir."

"Just look out, and if you see a gentleman on a black horse, ask him to ride close to the window, and not leave us, will you, and I'll give you a shill—I mean sixpence when we get to town. Look sharp out now. Bless me, Ealing Common! Why, there have been more robberies on Ealing Common lately than everywhere else put together. They say Sixteen-string Jack comes on this road sometimes, along with Claude Duval."

A slight start, and an exclamation from the young girl at his side, attracted the attention, not only of Tom Brereton, but of the other ladies as well.

"What alarms you?" said Cicely; and then,

darting a glance at her contemptible cousin, Tom Brereton, she added: "Pray, sir, keep your fears to yourself. We do not share them, and therefore cannot feel in any way interested in them. If we should be attacked by a highwayman, he will perhaps for a moment fancy we have a man to protect us; but he will soon find out his error."

"Ah!" said Tom, without showing much discomposure at the utterance of this remark, "I should not wonder now but you think you will put me quite in a pet by what you say, but, he—he—he! it won't do, I assure you. Oh, dear, no! And, besides, every inch that we get nearer town, there is less chance of a highwayman, and I, of course, am the more comfortable."

"Surely, sir," said the old lady, breaking silence, "you cannot mean that you have any serious intention of considering my son Markham as indebted to you for the use he has mistakenly made of the little property he thought belonged to us."

"Why, as to that, ma'am—aunt, I suppose I ought to call you—as to that, I——"

What sort of reply Mr. Tom Brereton was about to give to the remark of his aunt is most unfortunately lost to posterity, for at the moment when he had got so far in his speech, the carriage came to an abrupt halt, and a loud, clear voice from the roadside cried:

"Move another pace, postilion, and I will try the temper of your skull with a couple of slugs!"

"Murder!" groaned Tom Brereton, as according to his former expressed view of expediency in such a contingency, he slipped off his seat down among the straw at the bottom of the carriage. "Murder! There is a highwayman at last."

CHAPTER VI.

THE RECOGNITION—THE ROBBERY AND THE RESCUE—A NEW ACQUAINTANCE.

A SLIGHT cry of terror was all that came from the old lady, but Cicely, flinging her arms round her mother, said, with extraordinary courage:

"Be not alarmed—no man will wantonly injure us. I have heard that some of these highwaymen have chivalric notions of honour, where females are concerned."

"Oh, don't mention me to him, whatever you do," whined Tom Brereton. "Only think of my £20, my papers, and perhaps my life. Have mercy upon me! Confound the seat! I can't get under it. Miss Cicely—cousin Cicely, recollect we are cousins, you know. Oh, dear, here he comes!"

The side lamps of the carriage sent a halo of light around the vehicle, and by its assistance the occupants of the vehicle could see a man's face at one of the windows, which he rather dexterously let down from without, and then, in the softest and most winning accents, as he laid his hand upon the panel of the door, he said:

"Be not alarmed ladies, I beg I am aware

that there is an invalid here, and will do my spiriting gently. I have the honour to request your purses and watches."

"Spare our lives!" said the old lady.

"Lives! Oh, madam, can you fancy that I am a ruffian? I was misinformed, for a young gentleman, with whom I had the honour of a little conversation on the road, informed me that a man was of your party. You seem, however, to be alone. But do not let that circumstance alarm you. Unprotected females are the care of every gentleman."

"Will you permit us to pass, sir?" said Cicely.

"Certainly, miss, will I, after the little ceremony of exacting a slight tribute, since you are travelling over my territory. All monarchs must have supplies, you know, however much in this case I regret to see a shadow of alarm upon so lovely a face."

Cicely drew back as this compliment was uttered, for in her eagerness to endeavour to persuade the highwayman to allow them immediately to pursue their journey, she had brought one of the sweetest countenances the world ever saw within the sphere of the lamp-light, so that the highwayman caught a full sight of it, and he never forgot it.

"Take this," said the young girl, who had not yet spoken, as she handed a small silk purse to the robber. "Take this—look at it at your leisure, but leave us now."

"Who's that?" he cried. "Eh! Who spoke?"

As he uttered this hurried query, he looked more curiously into the carriage, the result of which was, that he saw the back of Mr. Tom Brereton's sky-blue coat.

"Hilloa! what have we here?" he added. "Any skulking, eh?"

With the butt-end of a large holster pistol, he dealt the hidden youth so sharp a blow that he rose with a howl of pain, crying:

"Oh, lor—oh, lor! Oh, my back! Have mercy upon me, good Mr. Highwayman, I'm only an unfortunate young man who has nothing to give you. If you please, sir, to let me go this time, I'll take care the next time I meet you to have a few pounds about me."

"Why, what poltroon is this?" cried the highwayman. "Come out, sir. Come out on to the common, and let me have a good look at you, that I may know a coward when I see one again. This fellow, ladies, is a disgrace to your society. Come out."

"Oh, dear me! Now, cousin Cicely, and you, aunt, and you, miss, what's your name, do say something for me, or I shall be murdered, I know. Oh, dear—oh, dear! Why did I come myself instead of sending somebody else on this errand?"

"Will you come out?"

"Don't insist upon it, I beg, sir, and I'll give you £10 down, upon my life I will."

"Be still, my 'Nell'!" said the highwayman to his horse, and then, immediately dismounting, he opened the door of the carriage, and seizing Mr. Tom Brereton by the collar, dragged him at once into the road, where that valorous individual fell upon his knees in the mud, and roared for mercy.

"Your money or your life!"

"Oh, yes, of course, sir. You will be paid. In this pocket-book is my money; I'll get it out, sir, in a moment. Thank you, sir, I'm very much obliged, indeed."

"There's no occasion for so much trouble," said the highwayman, as he twitched the pocket-book from the trembling hand of Tom. "I can take it out myself at my leisure."

"But, sir—good, kind, sir. There's all my papers there to prove who I am."

"Never mind, you are sure to gain by the exchange if you are taken for someone else! Ladies, have you any more money than what I have received?"

"We have but a small sum," said Cicely, "and Heaven knows how badly we want it."

"It is rather strange," replied the highwayman, "that ladies travelling in their own carriage should only have a small sum, and want that badly; but if you will tell me upon your honour that such is the case, I will take your word."

"Upon my honour it is so," said Cicely.

"That is sufficient; I have the honour, ladies, to wish you good-night."

Cicely's hand was upon the edge of the door, and before she could be aware of what he was about, the highwayman had raised it audaciously to his lips, and kissed it, adding, in a soft and most winning tone:

"Believe that there are worse folks on the road of life, who pass along unsuspected, than Claude Duval!"

"Claude Duval! Then you are that celebrated highwayman, who for the last year has filled report with his exploits, and—and—who——"

"Who never forgot that he was a gentleman in the presence of ladies," added the highwayman. "I have the honour to wish you good-night. You may pursue your journey in peace, but should you be stopped at Shepherd's Bush, just say that 'Nell' and her master have bidden you good-night, and you will be allowed to pass on unmolested."

With these words, the highwayman left the astonished travelling party, and springing upon the back of his horse, was in a moment lost in the gloom that was beyond the little circle of light, cast by the side-lamps of the carriage.

Mr. Tom was still in the mud, hardly able to believe that after all he had really escaped with his life, from what he considered the most terrible danger he had ever been in.

It was the postilion who first broke the silence that now ensued, and he did so by saying, in most dolorous accents:

"What shall I do, ladies? Shall I go on? It was no fault of mine, you know."

"Yes, yes," cried Cicely, "go on as quickly as you can."

"No, no," shouted Tom Brereton. "Stop a bit—stop a bit. Don't go without me; you forget that I was pulled out of the coach. Stop, I say! Don't be going on in that sort of way. Hilloa! I'm all over mud. Come, come, a joke's a joke, but this ain't one."

The postilion was glad to get on, and, in fact, before Tom had begun to call out in this way, on account of being left behind, the vehicle had already moved on a short distance, so that the terrified and bewildered postilion fully imagined that the shouting arose from other highwaymen, or perhaps the same, who might have come back, fancying he had not got enough out of the party.

The consequence of this was, that instead of stopping, he urged the horses on at increased speed, and after a futile attempt to hold on by the back of the carriage, Tom was left sprawling in the dirt.

Cicely knew very well that such a catastrophe had occurred, but she did not, under the circumstances, think there was any very urgent necessity for taking any steps to rectify it, and in a few minutes Tom was out of ear-shot.

As for the old lady, she was in such a state of fright, that she scarcely knew what had happened, while the younger girl, who had given the small purse to Claude Duval, uttered not a word.

Once Cicely thought she heard her weeping.

"Do not be alarmed, May," she said. "All is over now."

The young girl who was thus called May, started and spoke in a timid voice:

"Oh, yes, it is all over. Thank Heaven, it is all over, and he has taken nothing from any of you. Oh, most of all, I am deeply thankful for that. That is indeed a mercy."

"Nay, he could take but little from us, May, seeing that we have so little to lose, and certainly for a highwayman he was about as polite as anyone could possibly with any reason expect. I am most anxious about my brother, Markham, and fear that some evil has befallen him upon the road. You are weeping again, May."

"I am deeply affected."

"Nay, my dear May, you should not allow a little circumstance like this so to affect your nerves—all is over now."

"Can I be otherwise than affected," said the young girl, "when those who in my state of destitution gave me food and shelter, are exposed to danger? Was I not a wanderer without a home in the streets of London, when you and your dear, kind mother met me, and took me home with you?"

"Yes, but the candid manner in which you told us that you were an orphan, and that your name was May Russel, convinced us that we were right in thinking well of you, and your conduct has confirmed our judgment."

"Yes, yes, I told you my name was May Russel. Heaven will reward you."

"Say no more, May. This is a subject upon which you know I exacted, some time since, a promise that you would not speak. I knew all that you would say, and therefore exacted such a promise. Let me beg of you to keep it; but, be assured, that let our condition be what it may, and our means ever so

much reduced, you shall share with us what we have."

What reply the young girl would have made to this generous speech cannot be told, for the moment she was about to open her lips to speak, the carriage stopped, and the postilion, in a voice of terror, shouted:

"Oh, lor! here's another of 'em. I shall have them slugs in my nob yet, afore we gets to Tyburn Gate. Here's another!"

A horseman galloped up to the carriage, and in a clear voice, said:

"Ladies, have you been stopped by a highwayman to-night, for I have?"

"Yes, yes," said Cicely. "Yes."

"Probably, then, a little bead purse that I took from him belongs to one of you."

"Took from him!" cried the young girl who had been called May. "Have you—you killed him?"

"Oh, no. We had a little encounter, and I gained the victory, after which he said to me: 'I regret to say that I took from a young lady in a travelling carriage a little bead purse, with a small sum of money in it. Will you restore it for me as you are on the road, and are likely to see her?' Upon which I took it, and here it is. There are some very bad characters up the road by Shepherd's Bush, so, if you please, I will ride by the side of your carriage. I am well armed."

"Pray, sir, who are you?" said Cicely.

"I am an officer in the army, madam, but you see me in plain clothes, as I am at present what we call unattached."

The old lady had heard something of this colloquy, and at once proffered her thanks for the offer of the officer's protection to town, and after she had said that, Cicely did not know very well how to say anything to the contrary; although from the conduct of Claude Duval, she had no fear of a second attack from him; and, moreover, he had given her a pass-word against other depredators, in the efficacy of which she somehow or another placed implicit reliance, although coming from so suspicious a quarter as it did.

The officer now took it for granted that he had full power to consider himself the escort of the ladies, for he ordered the postilion to go on at an easy pace, and with his hand resting upon the window-sill of the carriage, he accommodated his horse's footsteps to those in the vehicle, and so was able to converse.

"And so you have been stopped," he said, "by the celebrated—perhaps I ought to say the notorious—Claude Duval?"

"Yes," said Cicely. "He told us that was his name."

"And of course then you met with much politeness. He is well known to be specially gallant to women—nay, I have been credibly informed in London that some ladies, who have been quite enchanted with the anecdotes told of the youthful gallant highwayman, have actually gone to Ealing Common for the sake of the chance of being stopped by him, and so achieving an interview with so celebrated a personage."

"Can it be possible?" said Cicely.

"Of my own knowledge, I cannot of course say, but I have heard as much."

"'Tis strange indeed," said Cicely. "We, on the contrary, were in much alarm."

"You should not travel on such roads as this unattended by a gentleman, permit me to say."

Cicely was about to make some remark about Tom Brereton, but she, upon a second thought, corrected herself, and said nothing in reply to the officer, who, after a pause, continued:

"It is, perhaps, not quite correct of me as a stranger to press my services upon you; but there is a frankness in your nature which will excuse me when I say that I should esteem it a high honour to be of service to you in London in any way. Pray pardon me for saying so much, if you should think it in the least impertinent."

"Nothing can be impertinent that is meant to be kind," said Cicely; "but we—we—must decline making acquaintance at present, sir."

"I bow to your decision," said the officer, "and as you will be soon in safety, I will leave you, merely remarking that I shall never forget this night."

"Indeed, sir!" said Cicely, in the most innocent manner in the world, for she was not sufficiently used to flattery to suspect that the stranger was only paving the way to the utterance of some well-turned compliment to her.

"Yes," he continued, "I shall cherish the remembrance of this brief conversation as one of the happiest moments of my life; I shall never forget tones that to my perception carry the sweetest music that my ears ever drank in with delight."

Cicely was silent—she felt hurt at this sudden freedom of the stranger's manner, and yet she did not know very well how to rebuke it, and he, probably fancying from her silence that he had a sort of licence to go on, added:

"We may never meet again, but be assured that not the most vivid scenes of a chequered existence can ever obliterate an image that now lies enshrined in my heart."

At this moment a troop of about eight horsemen came along the road from London, and the foremost of them called out to the officer:

"I beg your pardon, sir, but have you come far up the road with your friends in the coach?"

"Yes."

"Then, sir, have you had a tussle with any highwayman? We have come out to try if we can capture the celebrated Claude Duval. Our horses are good, and so is our will."

"It's a great pity you should be disappointed then, gentlemen, of a little sport. Ladies, I have the honour of bidding you good-night. Gentlemen, I am Claude Duval, and this is my mare, 'Nell.' Have you a mind for a canter to Wormwood Scrubs? If so, come on, and, as the old proverb says, 'the devil take the hindmost!'"

CHAPTER VII.

THE RACE—A WONDERFUL ESCAPE.

FOR a few moments, as might well be supposed, the horsemen who had so frankly announced their intention of capturing the highwayman, if they could, were so perfectly astounded at the cool assurance of the object of their attack, that he had got a considerable start before they could among them settle the question of pursuit or no pursuit.

One of the party, however, who was apt to be more prompt in his proceedings than the others, cried in a loud voice, as he spurred his horse:

"Forward! Do you want to be the laughing-stock of all London?"

In most critical circumstances there requires but someone to give an impulse, and in this case, as it does in almost all cases, it fully succeeded, for one and all, at the greatest speed their steeds could compass, dashed after the officer who had spoken.

But if the horsemen were astonished at finding the gentlemanly-looking man, whose occupation appeared to be that of escorting some ladies into town, turn out to be the celebrated Claude Duval, how much greater was the bewilderment and surprise of Cicely Brereton and her mother?

They were recalled, however, to a consciousness of the necessity of immediately proceeding, by the violent weeping of May, who sobbed with such convulsive energy that Cicely could not imagine why the occasion should be deemed sufficient to call forth such a gush of feeling, for, after all, singular as the adventure was, Cicely could find nothing affecting in it.

"My dear May," she said, "you have commonly so bold and firm a demeanour that I am surprised and grieved to find you thus affected."

"Then do not speak to me," said the young girl. "Do not speak to me just now, Miss Cicely; at another time perhaps I can tell you, but I implore you to ask me nothing."

This appeal, uttered in almost frantic accents, was more puzzling still, and it was something of a relief when the postilion cried out:

"Shall I drive on? I thought it was him, for I seed a bit of a red coat peeping out from under the cloak he had on. Oh, I thought it was him, all the while; but I daren't say nothing, or he'd pretty soon have settled me. Shall I go on now?"

"Yes, yes," said Cicely, "and as quickly as you can."

The carriage rattled onwards; but, as it will be far more interesting for us to follow Claude Duval down the western road, we will leave the ladies to take their way unmolested into London, and once more place ourselves upon the track of the highwayman.

Although Claude, with his usual daring recklessness had, as we have seen, invited a pursuit, he yet seemed to be doubtful if the

A HAIR-BREADTH ESCAPE.

challenge would, under the circumstances, be accepted by the horsemen, and as he was by no means inclined to be so absurd as to take a long gallop with no object, he reined in his horse, after going half-a-mile, and paused to listen.

All was still around him.

It seemed as if at that moment the very genius of silence had taken up its abode upon that spot of earth, and this solemn repose of nature would have had an effect upon the warm and not unsuperstitious mind of Duval, had he not been much more intensely occupied in listening for any sound indicative of pursuit.

And soon it came. He heard the heavy tread of horses' hoofs in full gallop.

"Ah, my 'Nell'!" he said, patting the neck of the beautiful animal he rode, "we shall be put upon our mettle. You must show them what blood can do with a light weight; and we must have no incumbrances, my lass."

As he spoke, he undid a clasp which held around his neck the cloak that had so effectually disguised him from the recognition of the ladies of the carriage, and slung the garment over the front of his saddle. He then shifted his hat round about, for he had changed it likewise for disguise, the hind part before, and then, with a low chirping whistle urged the horse forward, and off it went like the wind.

"My darling 'Nell'!" he muttered, "we could beat them on a fifty-mile chase, but why should we trouble ourselves to do so. We will bid them good-bye shortly, and if we can send them on a wild-goose chase, we will."

Again he held his head aside to listen, and his practised ear told him how much he gained upon his pursuers, and how easy a thing it would be to distance them completely, and then take a route across the country, instead of by the high road, and so baffle them all. But as these thoughts passed rapidly through his mind, he heard a horse approaching from the other direction at a sharp canter, which would soon bring its rider face to face with him.

This was not exactly what he wished, and yet it did not follow that the approaching horseman would take any notice of him, so he rode on, but at less speed, for he did not wish to seem to be a fugitive.

"Hold!" cried the horseman, as he came nearly up to Duval. "Hold, whoever you are, and answer me a question."

"What question?" said Duval, reining in 'Nell' so suddenly, that she reared, and would have thrown a less practised rider.

"Is your horse fresh?"

"As a daisy in April."

"Then you must exchange with me; I'm a king's messenger, and my horse is tired; I can convince you I am what I say I am by showing you the badge of my office—a silver hound. Come, dismount at once, or I must enforce my demand. If you attempt to escape, I shall send a pistol shot after you."

The king's messenger, for such he really was, spoke in a tone of decided and firm authority that would have awed many a man into compliance with his wishes, especially as it was well known that ample remuneration was always given in such cases; but if ever a bold man met his match, the messenger did when he encountered Claude Duval.

"It's very kind of you," said Claude, as the messenger flung himself off his horse, and came towards him with the bridle in his hand, "to tell me who you are, and I cannot think of being otherwise than equally candid."

"Pho! pho! dismount, sir."

"I am Claude Duval, the highwayman."

"The devil!"

"No, only one of his messengers. Good-night."

As he uttered these words, Claude twitched the bridle of the messenger's horse out of his hand, and giving the rein to "Nell," he was off, with the other steed dashing on by his side, at the full stretch of the bridle which he held it by.

This transaction had occupied far less space in the enacting than in the telling, and the galled and bewildered messenger found himself in the middle of the road, nearly five miles from London, and without a horse at all, in addition to which his own horse, when it

plunged off in obedience to the impulse given it by Claude Duval, had saluted its former master with a kick, which, although not very serious, made him glad to sit down by the side of the road, feeling a little sick and uncomfortable.

In another moment the troop of horsemen in pursuit of Duval swept past the unfortunate king's messenger at full speed, paying no attention to the cry he raised for aid.

On dashed Claude, and the horse without a rider, being relieved from its load, kept up the speed well which "Nell" enforced; but yet amused as he was by this little extra adventure, Claude began to think he had better get rid of his captured steed, and he was upon the point of casting the bridle from him, when he heard a voice cry:

"Murder! Murder! Will no Christian help me? Oh, murder; murder! I'm all alone; I've been robbed by a highwayman. My name's Tom Brereton—murder! Help! Help!"

This was the very spot where he, Duval, had first stopped the carriage, and he at once knew that the person who called so energetically for assistance, was the young man whom he had dragged out of the vehicle by the collar.

His fertile imagination and love of frolic at once suggested to him a plan of baffling his pursuers without fatiguing "Nell," which he immediately resolved to put into practice.

"Oh, sir," he cried, "have you been robbed by a highwayman?"

"Yes, yes. Oh, dear; yes, and ill-treated, too."

"Well, I can tell you that there is on this road to-night a regular gang of highwaymen, who are determined to rob and murder everybody they meet. This is my master's horse that I am leading, mount it, and gallop on—keeping the high road, mind—till you meet a party of dragoons who are coming from Brentford, and then you will be safe; but if you or I remain longer here our throats will be cut."

"Oh, indeed—you don't say so."

"Indeed I do, though. Come, quick, mount. I'll help you. Hold on anyhow, by his ears and his mane, for if you fall off you are lost. There, take this cloak, wrap it round you, I'll clasp it—no thanks—all's right, off with you. Don't leave the high road. Quick, I hear them coming! Don't say a word; of course we ought all to help each other at a pinch."

"Oh, dear—oh, dear. I can't ride."

"Hold on, anyhow, I tell you, and fancy all the while you feel a knife sawing away at your throat."

"Gracious goodness! Murder!"

Claude Duval gave the horse a slashing blow with his riding-whip, and off it went, nearly maddened by pain and excitement, carrying Tom Brereton at a reckless pace, while the cloak that was clasped round his neck floated behind him. like some victorious banner.

"Now, my 'Nell,'" said Duval, and, springing into the saddle again, he turned the creature's head towards a hedge by the roadside, which she, fully understanding what was required of her, cleared beautifully, alighting softly in a meadow on the opposite side, when Claude again immediately dismounted.

"Down, girl—down," he said, and the horse crouched to its knees, and then lay upon its side as quiet as possible, while Claude crouched likewise to the ground, for there was behind them a patch of light-coloured sky, against which he and the horse might, perchance, have been seen.

It was well that not a moment had been lost, for scarcely had these precautions for concealment been taken, when the pursuing party came up, and actually paused for a moment on that spot.

"He has taken to the meadows, I think," said one.

"No, no," shouted he who was heading the pursuit. "I saw his cloak fluttering behind him on the brow of the hill there, just as you get into Acton, by Berrymead Priory. Come on. Come, we shall have him yet. Come on."

Away they went again, and were soon lost to sound as well as to sight.

"So you think you will have him, do you?" laughed Claude Duval. "No, no; my time has not come yet. Well, well, I have not had much luck to-night, so I will to London, and look over the pocket-book belonging to that cowardly fellow, Tom Brereton, who, I suppose, will not stop until his horse falls with him. I can't get that girl, Cicely, out of my head. How came May to be with them?"

CHAPTER VIII.

THE "OLD MOON" IN GATE STREET—A CHANCE SHOT—A VISITOR TO CLAUDE.

In Gate Street, Lincoln's Inn Fields, there was a public-house called the "Old Moon." It has been long since swept away, and nothing even to indicate the site of it now remains.

At the period of our story, however, it was in a flourishing condition, and was kept by a man whom no one ever knew by any other name than that of Anthony.

He was a tall, lank, straight-haired, methodistical-looking fellow, and had a way of turning up his eyes, and uttering pious ejaculations, as if he were the most religious person in the whole neighbourhood; and, truly, if attending a meeting-house in Little Queen Street, and being about as hypocritical a rascal as ever stepped, gave him any claims to that character, he certainly fulfilled it.

At two o'clock on the eventful night, some of the particulars of which we have brought before the reader, Anthony sat dozing in his bar.

To be sure, his house was shut, to all appearances, but at its back there was a long, low-roofed room, to which there was an entrance by the flap of a cellar, down a stable-yard, and there Anthony had still some customers, although the hour was rather a late, or rather, we ought, perhaps, to say, an early one.

These customers of Anthony's were of a peculiar description, for at one end of the long room sat a man behind a kind of counter, and almost everybody who entered went up to him and placed some article in front of him, at which he invariably shook his head in disapproval and contempt. He would then hand out some money, which operation was almost invariably accompanied by a declaration that he was ruining himself—by degrees—always by degrees.

The articles so bought were then placed in a basket, which projected from the wall behind him, and, whenever he had a small lot collected, he gave some sort of signal, and the basket disappeared. It was connected with a turnabout similar to what may be seen in many convent-gates on the Continent; and, after a few moments, it was sent back empty by the same means.

At the other entrance to the room, two men and two dogs kept watch and ward. No one was permitted to enter who was unknown to one or the other of them, so that the place was tolerably well guarded from intrusion.

"I shall be ruined—by degrees," said the man at the counter, as he swept away another supply of valuables. "Ah, Poll!" he added in an altered tone, "is that you, my lass? If I were not being ruined—by degrees—you should have a glass of the best wine in Anthony's cellar."

"Yes," said the girl, smiling through her tears, for her face and eyes were swollen by violent weeping, "by degrees, I suppose. Where is Claude to-night?"

"Ah, my dear, that's what I have been asking; but business has fallen off dreadfully of late. I have known the time when Sixteen-string Jack would bring——"

"He's in Newgate now," interrupted the girl, with a burst of sobs; "where we shall all go in time."

"Ahem! yes—by degrees. And so Jack is in Newgate?"

"Yes; and he will go to Tyburn to-morrow."

"By degrees, I suppose he will. Upon my life it's a pity, a great pity, when you come to think of it—by degrees. Don't you think it is, Poll?"

"Don't bother; I want to see Claude. Don't you know he vowed to Jack that he would meet him on his road to Tyburn, and shake hands with him, in spite of all the officers."

"Why, a—yes—by degrees."

"Well, I've seen Jack, and he tells me that there will be such an attempt to take Claude if he shows himself to-morrow, that he had better not do so. Jack says he'll excuse him, and begs me to ask him, in the name of their old friendship, not to try it. I thought to have found him here. I'll go and speak to Anthony, perhaps he knows where he is. They say that six officers to-morrow are to share £200 among them if they take Claude."

The girl seemed well acquainted with the place, for after this brief dialogue with the man at the counter, she opened a door at one corner of the room, which disclosed a small flight of dark stairs; but while she is seeking Anthony, we will attend to something of rather an interesting nature which is going on just outside the entrance to the stable-yard, from which opened the cellar entrance of the "Old Moon."

Two men were standing in the deep shadow of a small doorway opening into one of the stables which happened to be untenanted, and they were conversing in whispers.

"It was all very well," said one of them, "to draw lots in the Governor's house at Newgate, as to which six of the lot of us should take Claude Duval to-morrow, if he ventures upon coming to shake hands with Sixteen-string Jack, and share the £200 among them; but as we were not lucky enough to belong to the lot, it ain't so pleasant to see our £33 a piece go by us, is it now?"

"Sartinly not; but what a do it will be if we grabs him to-night, won't it?"

"Rather, I should say. Do you think the girl Lucy's information is to be depended on, that he get's here at half-past two or so, and remains till the next evening?"

"Yes, I do. Claude will have nothing to say to her, and a spiteful woman, you know, will do anything."

"Very good, now you know what we are to do. If he comes, I am to get behind him, and fling my arms round him, while you, under threat of blowing his brains out, pop on the darbies."

"All's right. I don't see the trouble of taking him. He's only one, after all. It's people giving him an advantage by being afraid that does the business."

"Yes, that's it. Well, you remain where you are, and I'll get on the other side of the gateway. Don't you move till you see my arms round him, and now, as we are in a queer neighbourhood, the less we say the better."

While this conversation was taking place, a figure, muffled up very much about the face, came at a rapid pace down Queen Street, and just as it was about to cross towards Gate Street, a girl rushed out of a doorway, and flung herself at its feet.

"Claude, Claude!" she said. "Is it you, Claude?"

"Lucy!" said Claude Duval, for it was indeed he. "What ails you?"

"Kill me—oh, kill me, Claude; you ought to kill me."

"I kill you, Lucy?" exclaimed Claude, in the utmost surprise. "Why, you must be dreaming, or have you taken leave of your senses?"

"I don't know—I don't know!" she cried, in distracted tones; "but when you treated me so coldly—when you would not speak to

me, or even see me, if you could help it, it drove me mad! It made me hate you, and—and I—I have betrayed you!"

"Betrayed me?" ejaculated Claude, starting back.

"Yes—yes. Now kill me, Claude—you see now you must kill me! I shall die happy, but let my last words be, *Don't go to the 'Old Moon' to-night.*"

But by this time Claude had recovered his ordinary composure, and he raised the half-crazy girl to her feet.

"What have you done that should prevent me going to-night to the 'Old Moon'? Come into this doorway, and tell me what all this means. Are you mad?"

"Mad—mad! Yes, that must be it. In a fit of madness—in a moment of despair and rage, I told an officer named Morgan that you were in the habit of visiting the 'Old Moon' at about this hour. Kill me now, and I will not blame you, for you cannot forgive me!"

"Oh, yes, I can easily and do. Thanks for your warning. Good-night."

The girl sank back in the doorway, and gasped out—

"You are too good—too generous. But where are you going now?"

"Now? Why, to the 'Old Moon,' of course."

"No—no. You must not—you shall not!"

"Enough," said Claude, abruptly. "For your timely warning, many thanks. I go now. Farewell!"

He strode on quickly as he spoke.

"Is the girl mad, indeed?" he muttered. "Well, probably I do not encounter more danger by going to the 'Old Moon' now than I run into almost every hour of my life. Besides, to tell the truth, I am a little curious to know how Morgan will manage this affair. My principal safety comes from the cupidity of the officers. They will not combine to take me, because each individual's share of the reward is not sufficient to induce him to participate in the danger, so I am pretty safe, after all."

He looked carefully to his weapons, and held himself prepared for any sudden attack that might be made upon him.

Of course, it was not an attempt upon his life that he had to fear, but his liberty, and it was this consideration, doubtless, that gave him a kind of fearlessness which, if his destruction had been aimed at, he could not possibly have possessed, for then he would not have known at what moment a pistol-shot might have put an end to his career.

As it was, however, he passed on with an appearance of composure to the gateway leading to the stables, where his two enemies were posted.

He wisely kept in the middle of the entry, and he had passed on some few steps, when, according to his plan—which was no bad one—Morgan dashed out, and clasped him from behind, round the body, missing the arms, however, which it had been his great object to secure.

"Now, Bill," he cried, "now for the darbies. We have him. It's a hundred pounds a-piece."

"Perhaps a small part of an ounce will do for one of you," said Claude, as, snatching a pistol from his belt, he fired it at the open doorway in front of him, where he had just seen the glance of the other officer's eyes, as he was preparing to spring out.

A shriek mingled itself with the report of the pistol, and, at the same moment, by a dexterous twist of one of his legs, Claude flung the officer who had hold of him on his back; but he would not loose his hold, and Claude went with him, but uppermost, of course, so that while the officer got a blow upon the back of his head on the curbstones, he, Claude, was quite uninjured, and, finding that his opponent was insensible, he rose in a moment.

"So, so," he said. "That was the plan, was it? Not a bad one, either, Master Morgan; it only wants the one condition of success to be entitled to great praise. Ha! who comes here? Stand, or you die!"

"'Tis I, Claude," said Lucy. "I could not leave you."

"Eh? what's all this?" said old Anthony, the publican, who had been roused by the report of the pistol, and guessed that some of his customers were in trouble. "The Lord look down upon us—amen. What's the row, eh, my rummy one?"

"Nothing particular," said Claude.

"Eh? What? Why it's you, Duval. Let us pray—I mean come in, my tulip. Have the grabs been at you? Come along, my daffy-down-dilly, come along."

"No," said Claude; "I only want to know if you have any news for me, Anthony?"

"Yes, I have. Here's Poll has just come from Sixteen-string Jack, and he says you had better leave him alone to-morrow, for the Philistines will be mighty, and are determined, the Lord willing, to have you."

"Oh, is that all?"

"Yes; and enough, too. But who fired the shot I heard just now?"

"No matter about that. When I am gone, bring a lantern, and look about you; but tell Poll to say to Jack, when she sees him in the morning, that I'll shake hands with him, according to my promise, come what may of it. I have said it, and Claude Duval never broke his word yet."

"Amen!" said Anthony. "I shall go in to prayers. Good-night, Claude, and luck go with you, for you are as fine a fellow as ever stepped, only I never could awaken you to a proper sense of religion. I'll come out with a lantern, and look about, as you say. I suppose somebody is in trouble."

"Not at all," said Claude. "Somebody's troubles are over, probably. Good-night! I must seek another shelter, Anthony, though I have much to do before morning."

"Good-night; and give up your harebrained scheme."

"Never! When I was friendless and homeless, Jack was kind to me, and I then said, in answer to a remark of his, that some day he should swing at Tyburn; but let that day—which I hoped was far distant—come when it would, I would meet him on the road to the triple tree, and, in spite of all, would clasp his hand in mine, and call him my friend."

"It's certain death to attempt it!" said old Anthony, who, in his excitement, forgot to employ his usual canting phraseology. "Give it up. Even Jack himself has sent word that you are not to attempt it."

"That makes no difference. Say no more, Anthony; but, good-night. The danger is not so great as you think it, and, besides, I shall take all the precautions I can. In a life like mine, daring carries such a charm along with it, that it saves me from a thousand little risks which otherwise would swarm about me if it was once thought I feared them!"

CHAPTER IX.

THE PROMISE FULFILLED—THE ROUTE TO TYBURN.

A DRIZZLY, misty rain began to fall, wrapping all London in a dense mantle of chilling fog. By day-break the only difference from the night was, that the wet mist, which had before looked black, now wore a dingy grey aspect, through which the few passengers who were abroad loomed like spectres.

The rain streamed down the front of Newgate in long, black streaks, taking the channels of old streams, and falling with a dull, pattering sound upon the pavement beneath—a sound which, slight as it was, had reached the ears of a man who was to be hanged at Tyburn at twelve o'clock next day.

That man was Sixteen-string Jack.

He had passed rather a wakeful night, but, as he washed his face the next morning, he whistled a popular air in a loud key while he looked at the turnkey who had brought him the means wherewith to make his ablutions.

"What time is it?"

"Nearly nine," said the turnkey. "Would you like anything, Jack?"

"Yes, I should. Get me a lot of stewed oysters. They always make me ill in a few hours after taking them; but I shall be dancing on nothing at twelve o'clock, and then it won't matter, and, I say—has Poll been again this morning? I want to see her."

"No, Jack, she hasn't been. I knows what you wants to see her for. It's to ask her if she has told Claude Duval not to try to shake hands with you in the cart. You may depend she has ferreted him out, and he'll not be so mad as to try it on, surely, when he knows that there's £200 issued out agin him."

Jack shook his head.

"I'm afraid," he said, "I'm very much afraid he'll try it. Claude doesn't look at danger beforehand, and when it comes he

stares it out of countenance. If there were
£2,000 against his name he would not mind.
He gave his hand to me upon the promise a
year ago, and he'll keep his word. It's the
only thing that gives me an uncomfortable
feeling to-day. They will nab poor Claude, as
safe as possible. I'm afraid of that, and
nothing else."

"Perhaps he won't try it on, after all,
Jack."

"I'm afraid he will. But, however, as the
old song says, 'What's the use o' grieving.'
I will hope for the best, if I think the worst.
I suppose we shall start soon—what noise is
that?"

"The cart, Jack, that's all. There's a
thousand people outside Newgate now, and
they are pouring in by all the thoroughfares
as fast as nothing."

"I wish Poll would come. Where can she
be? I suppose they will let her past the
gate. It's very odd she isn't here, and nine
o'clock, too. Who's that coming?"

"Mr. Needles, the sheriff, Jack."

Mr. Needles was the most bandily-shaped
man that the imagination could picture, for,
being just about as broad as he was long, he
might have been set up in any way without
detriment to his appearance, always providing
that his sheriff's gown and chain were disposed accordingly.

He was very near-sighted, too, so that,
when he wished to see anybody, he had to
come within an inch of his nose; but he was
a kind-hearted man, and, whenever there was
an execution, his feelings used to put him into
such a state of perspiration that he shone all
over his face and round, bald head, like a
double dip in July. It was his duty, now, to
let the prisoner know that he would soon have
to bid the world adieu.

"Ahem!" he said. "Mr. a—a—really, I
don't know your right name—Mr. a—a—a."

"Call me Jack, sir—call me Jack. You
have done several kind things since I have
been here, and I thank you with all my
heart."

"Oh, don't mention that," said Mr. Needles,
getting more shiny than before. "Dear me,
I often wish I was not a sheriff, but my time
will soon be out, that's one comfort. Well,
Jack—since that's what I am to call you—I
have only to say that we start at ten, you
know, from here. Bless me, what's that?"

"Something among the crowd outside,
sir," said an official. "Hilloa! Davis, what's
all that shouting for outside?"

"Only a mad bull, sir, among the people,"
said Davis.

"Poll not come," said Jack. "Poll not
come!"

"You won't see her this morning, Jack,"
said the turnkey. "A man on a *hellephant*,
and in armour, couldn't get through such a
crowd as there is now outside of Newgate, so
it's quite out of the question."

"Well," said Jack, with a sigh, "I suppose
it can't be helped. Mr. Needles, it won't be
fair at all to interfere with Claude Duval to-

day, when, if he comes at all to the cart-side,
it will only be to make an old friend's heart
lighter by shaking hands with him as he goes
to death. It will be a dastardly thing to interfere with him then, sir."

"Dear me," said the little fat sheriff, "you
know I have no more to do with that than the
man in the moon, Jack; I can't help it. It's
uncommonly absurd of him to come if he don't
want to be caught."

"It is, but Claude is the man to do it for all
that, and glory in it. I'm sorry Poll can't get
to tell me if she took him my message. Ah!"

The great bell of Newgate had begun to
toll. The sheriff took out an amazing hand-
kerchief, and wiped his head and face, which
process took some of the shine off it for a
time, and then he bustled out of the cell just
as a turnkey ran in with some stewed oysters
for Jack, according to the request he had made
for that delicacy.

It was not any personal fear of his approaching death at Tyburn that made Jack turn
aside, and shake his head at the stewed
oysters: it was his dread, lest Claude Duval
should be taken in his hare-brained attempt to
shake hands with him, that unmanned him.

"No, no," he said, "I thank you all the
same; it was kind of you, and while I live I
am not likely to forget it. Good-bye, old
fellow. You are among the few that I would
have liked to stay among yet awhile, but as it
can't be, why it can't, and there's an end of it.
I'm wanted, I suppose."

"Yes, Jack. They are waiting to knock
your irons off."

"Very good, I'm ready."

A sort of procession escorted Jack to the
lobby, where the process of knocking off his
irons was adroitly performed, and then, while
a strange murmur arose from the crowd, partly
of sympathy, and partly of excitement, the
condemned man was placed in the cart that
was ready to convey him to the place of execution.

Jack was bare-headed, and his face was
pale, while his eyes roved over that sea of
faces as if with intense anxiety, looking for
someone whom he wished to recognize.

The chaplain got into the cart, and shook
his head in a manner which he intended
should be impressive, and strike the crowd
with a solemn awe, but the only effect it had
was to elicit an inquiry from one of the nearest
spectators if he shook his head because he
thought there was anything in it.

This produced a laugh, but that soon passed
off as the pale, anxious countenance of Sixteen-string Jack, and his roving eyes, met the
people's gaze.

Just as the cart was about to start, and at
least a couple of dozen of persons, who had
pressed forward eagerly to offer drink, or to
shake hands with the culprit, had been thrust
back by the officers, the Governor of Newgate
stepped up to the cart with an open letter in
his hand, and, leaning forward to Jack, said:

"A quaker gentleman, of the name of Luke
Houlditch, living at Tottenham, and who was

robbed on the highway by some one near Finchley, about three months ago, has written to say that if you will declare whether it was you or not, probably it will ward off suspicion from another person who is suspected. Have you any objection?"

"Surely not at such a time as this," said the chaplain.

"None in the least," said Jack. "Can't he come and identify me. I can hardly take upon myself, with any certainty, to say yes or no, unless he does."

"He says he thinks he should know you, but that he dreads a crowd. However, he will make an endeavour to see you as you proceed up Oxford Street, when he hopes you will satisfy him, and I see no harm in your doing so."

Jack placed his hand upon his forehead for a moment, and then, as a flush of colour came across his face, no one knew why, he said:

"Be it so; let him come and look at me if he likes. I care for no man's scrutiny now."

"Very well. Officers, you will not obstruct Mr. Houlditch if he should make his appearance; I know the name well at Tottenham, as that of a wealthy and most respectable gentleman. Good-bye, Jack. I hope you have had nothing to complain of since you have lodged with me?"

"Nothing, sir," said Jack. "Good-day—we shall have some more rain, I think."

The Governor drew back, and the cart started.

CHAPTER X.

CLAUDE'S DANGER—THE RIOT AND THE ESCAPE—THE EXECUTION.

THE moment the cart began to move there was a terrific rush among the crowd to accompany it as closely as possible, and those who from an early hour had taken up their stations near the fatal vehicle had much difficulty in maintaining their places.

Blows were freely exchanged on all sides, numbers of people were knocked down in the muddy street, and trampled upon without mercy; and it was not until Holborn Bridge was gained that anything like order was restored, and then it was the order of confusion.

Ballad-singers bawled themselves hoarse in singing the exploits, real and fictitious, of the hero of the day, while twenty voices at once would sometimes shout to Sixteen-string Jack words of admonition and encouragement regarding his behaviour at the scaffold.

The procession consisted of about twenty-six police officers, six of which number, it was remarked, kept much together, and seemed like men whose minds were made up to some rather hazardous and ticklish adventure.

Those were the six who hoped to share amongst them the reward for the capture of Claude Duval, if he should be daring enough to make his appearance in conformity with the promise he had made to Sixteen-string Jack; and that such a person as the celebrated Claude Duval had made such a promise materially augmented the crowd, for many persons came miles on purpose to catch a glimpse of a highwayman whose romantic exploits had in one short twelve months filled so much the ear of fame, of course gathering much from popular exaggeration.

Slowly the procession made its way up Holborn Hill, amid all the discordant cries incidental to such an exhibition, and there was no pause until St. Giles's was reached, when, according to custom, a flagon of ale was handed to the condemned man.

Jack just tasted it with his lips, and motioned the driver of the cart to go on.

It was evident to all who saw him, that as the procession turned into Oxford Street, an expression of great concern came over his face, and he looked more anxious than before.

The officers, too, as they marked this change in his aspect, moved closer around the cart, and kept a most vigilant eye upon their prisoner.

In this way the strange and heterogeneous cavalcade reached a cluster of houses, at the back of which was Swallow Street, and to which extinct thoroughfare a paved court led.

At the head of this court was a man upon a black horse, who seemed to be saying something in a quiet way to a jeering mob that was around him.

The clothing of the horseman was of grey serge, of the true quaker's cut, and he wore a broad-brimmed felt hat.

"I tell thee, friends," he said, in a nasal voice, "that I have travelled even from Tottenham High Cross, to see this sinner and man of violence, for have I not suspected my own man, Choppings, of waylaying me, and did I not likewise suspect the slaughterer of animals, commonly called a butcher, Dobbs, who resideth at Tottenham, likewise of being the culprit, and have I not, with the strong arm of the law, prosecuted him?"

"What will you take for your hat, friend?" cried a voice in tolerable imitation of the quaker.

"Something of more worth than thy wit, friend," replied the man of peace.

A roar of laughter followed this retort, and another man cried:

"Can't you let the poor fellow go to Tyburn in peace?"

"Yea, friend, truly I do not wish otherwise: but if I recognize in him the son of Belial, who robbed me upon the highway, and he confesseth so much upon seeing me, verily, you see, I shall cease from suspecting and prosecuting innocent people; but should he say unto me, truly, friend Houlditch, I did not rob thee, and strike thee upon the nose——"

Another scream of laughter drowned the quaker's voice.

"Yea and verily, friends," added Mr. Houlditch, "I say unto ye, that my nose swelled exceedingly from the blow stricken thereon."

"Serve you right, too," cried a fellow.

"Thou mayest possibly be right, friend. The only bad thing is that thou art not served right by divers strokes on thy back at the cart's tail, as thou hast more than once already experienced."

It was quite clear that the mob was no match in wit for the quaker, so no one tried any more attacks upon him. Moreover, the procession was now close at hand, and that concentrated all the interest of the scene.

"Come out, broad-brim," said one; "here's Jack coming."

"Yea, and so am I, friend. I only placed myself under this balcony, lest my outward man should get wet by the rain, which is even now coming down. I fear that I shall not be able to get to him, as I am a man of peace and little used to pushing and shouting, verily."

"Make way for the quaker!" cried several. "Make a passage for old broad-brim and no whiskers!"

"I thank thee, friend; but if thou hadst no whiskers, thy wife, who is strong in the flesh, could not pull them."

"Confound the fellow!" muttered the man. "He has his answers always ready."

The exclamations of the mob, and the odd figure of the quaker on horseback, attracted the attention of the officers who were surrounding the cart, and they judged at once that he was the Mr. Houlditch who had been spoken of by the Governor of Newgate, and as he was upon the near side of the way, there was no great difficulty in inclining the cart towards the pavement so that he might ask his question of Sixteen-string Jack.

The demeanour of Jack now filled everyone with surprise, for he betrayed much agitation of manner. His colour went and came, and he opened and shut his hands, while he muttered some words to himself, the only one of which that could be caught was "reckless."

The cart was stopped within half-a-dozen paces of the pavement, and with great difficulty, through the throng of people, the quaker made his way on his horse towards it, while Sixteen-string Jack looked eagerly at him.

"Now, sir," cried one of the officers; "ask your questions, and have done with it."

"What a throat thou hast got, friend," said the quaker; "keep thy mouth shut, I pray thee."

"Hoorah! Hoorah!" shouted the crowd, and various expressions indicative of a growing admiration for friend Houlditch were freely uttered, while the officer who had spoken so roughly, bit his lips with vexation.

"And so," said Houlditch, to the condemned man, "thou art Sixteen-string Jack?"

"Yes," said Jack, and his voice faltered as he spoke; "yes, and it's come to this at last."

"Well, friend, now I look thee in the face, I declare thou did'st never wrong me."

"Bravo—bravo!" cried a great blacksmith,

who was close at hand. "Bravo! This here quaker is a trump!"

"Give me thy hand, Sixteen-string Jack," added Houlditch. "God bless thee, my poor fellow! God bless thee!"

"God bless you," said Jack, and tears gushed to his eyes.

"By Heaven, I suspect——" cried a mounted officer, making a grasp at the quaker.

"What?" said Houlditch, as with one blow of the heavy loaded end of his riding-whip, he knocked the officer senseless from his horse. "Suspect what, fool? Not more than I am quite willing to avow."

He threw off the broad-brimmed hat as he spoke, and Jack cried:

"Fly, fly. Oh, fly!"

"Claude Duval!" cried a hundred voices.

"Yes," shouted the sham quaker, in a voice that made itself loudly and clearly heard above all other sounds. "Yes, I am Claude Duval, and I have redeemed my promise, of taking a last farewell of my old, kind friend, and bidding God bless him."

The officers made a dash at Claude; but the people, with a roar of determination, closed around him, and the great blacksmith shouted:

"Don't let them have him. Claude Duval never took a sixpence from a poor man in all his life, though he has given many a one."

"Fly! fly!" again cried Jack.

A shower of stones saluted the officers, and the chaplain fell down flat in the bottom of the cart, to get out of the danger of the missiles.

Everything seemed to promise that a severe contest between the officers and the populace would ensue, and the former drew their staves; but as they were greeted by a laugh of derision, pistols were produced.

"We will have him, dead or alive!" said one.

"Take him then," said Claude. "Farewell, Jack. I have kept my word."

"Nobly—nobly!" said Jack. "And—and Poll?"

"Shall never want while Claude has a crust to share with her, Jack. Make your mind easy about her. Good-bye."

Some of the crowd had pressed Claude's horse on to the pavement, and a lane was made for him, while the officers were so seriously obstructed that they could not move an inch; but two of the horsemen had cutlasses, and they began to use them upon the heads of the people so furiously that the mob gave way a little, and unfortunately for Claude, he had just arrived opposite the opening of a street, from which a dense mass of people came rushing to know what had happened, so that he was completely fixed, while the officers were now gradually nearing him.

At the corner of the street was a shop of some sort, but it had been closed to avoid danger to the windows, and above the shop was a large balcony, in front of the windows on the first floor.

Suddenly one of these windows opened, and

a girl of great beauty rushed into the balcony.

"Claude! Claude!" she cried; "it is Claude. Oh, Heaven, 'tis he."

Claude Duval glanced at the window, and the words, "My sister May," escaped his lips.

The mob, too, heard the young girl's exclamation, and the blacksmith shouted:

"Can you take him in at the window, miss? If you don't, he'll swing at Tyburn this day week."

"Yes, yes. Oh, yes, anything. Claude—Claude!"

Duval himself saw that this was now his only chance of escape, and, with surprising agility, he rose in the saddle, and stood on the back of the horse, by which means he was enabled to clutch the lower rails of the balcony. In another moment he drew himself up, and, waving his hand, disappeared in at the window of the house, which was shut, and the shutters closed immediately.

The mob gave three terrific cheers to express its triumph at the escape of the man, who, for the moment, in consequence of a chivalrous act, had become its idol.

The victim had escaped, but the confusion was still most serious.

The officers dismounted, for the purpose of breaking in the door of the house in which Duval had taken refuge; but that turned out to be a foolish proceeding, for being now on foot, they were much more on an equality with the mob, and it was only by abandoning the siege of the house, that they regained their steeds.

They held a short consultation among themselves.

"What's to be done?" cried one. "Are we to lose the money?"

"Certainly not. But, you see, we shall get pulled to pieces by the mob if we make any attack upon the house. We must go on to Tyburn now."

"And do you think that Claude Duval will wait for us until we get back? That's a likely thing."

"No. I never expected any such thing; but I propose that we go on a little way, as if we had completely given up all idea of taking him, and then that two of us, with as little observation as possible, detach ourselves from the cavalcade, and go back to watch the house he has taken refuge in, so that if he does go from it, at all events he can be dogged."

"It's the only thing that can be done. Come along."

When the people saw the officers were consulting, and casting angry glances up at the house where Claude had found an asylum, they fully expected that some immediate and violent attack would be made upon it; but when the procession moved on to Tyburn, and no further notice of the affair was taken, the populace raised a great shout of derision, and the blacksmith cried out:

"Three cheers for Claude Duval," which were given most heartily.

We need not pursue the catastrophe at Tyburn, further than to say that Sixteen-string Jack, with all his faults, failings, crimes, and virtues, suffered the dreadful death that had been inflicted on so many—innocent we conscientiously believe as well as guilty—at that fatal spot, which, even now when its name is mentioned, fills the imagination with fearful recollections of the past.

The lifeless body hung its hour, and was then removed by two females, who brought a hackney-coach to take the sad remains, and their talk—for talk they did even amid their tears as they went away—was as much of the chivalrous Claude Duval and of his ultimate fate, as of him whom, in silence for ever, they had with them as a horrible and ghastly companion.

The officers did not forget their scheme of separating two of their number from the main body, secretly to watch the house in Oxford Street, where Claude had so very opportunely found shelter, and so intent were the multitude upon the last moments of Sixteen-string Jack, that the manœuvre was executed without exciting observation.

It would, however, have taken more wit and more courage than belonged to all the officers put together to have circumvented Claude Duval. His time had not yet come, and he was doomed to be the hero of yet more striking adventures than any that had hitherto fallen to his lot.

We will take a glance at him.

CHAPTER XI.

THE INTERVIEW BETWEEN THE BROTHER AND SISTER—THE TITLE DEEDS—CLAUDE'S DESPAIR.

IT was, indeed, no other than poor May—of whom the reader has latterly had but a transient glimpse—who assisted her brother Claude in at the window of the house in Oxford Street.

For the first time during two years, he felt the pressure of her hand in his, and as the rapidly closed casement and shutters stilled the roar of the multitude without, he could hear the sobs that came from her agonized heart.

All was darkness, however, now in the room, for the shutters were hastily barred by May, and, fitting closely as they did, scarcely a ray of daylight found its way into the apartment. How complete—how total was the change from the shouts of the multitude without, and the glare of midday, to the silence and darkness of that room!

Claude was sensibly affected by it, and his voice shook as he spoke to his sister.

"You have saved me, May," he cried.

"Hush. Oh, hush," she said. "This way—this way."

She opened a door, and a gleam of light came again into the room.

He followed her into an apartment at the back of the house, and then she tried to look at him—she took his hand and strove to speak, but the effort was too great, and, bursting into tears, she flung herself upon a couch in an agony of grief.

Claude shook a little, and he paced the room several times before he spoke.

Then, pausing opposite to May, he strove to assume a calm and composed voice, as he reiterated:

"May, you have saved my life."

"And you, Claude," she sobbed, "have broken my heart."

"Is this kind, May, at such a time as this?"

"Kind! Oh, Claude—Claude, can you utter a reproach? What are you? Dare I answer my own question. You were poor, forlorn, dejected; what are you now?"

"None of those, May."

"Worse, worse—a thousand times worse—for you then stood upon a rock of adamant, you sat upon a throne, before which angels might bow down in reverence."

"You speak in riddles, May. I must confess my inability to understand you."

"The rock you stood upon, and the throne upon which nature had placed you, have both one name. That name is innocence."

"Let others upbraid me for my life," he said, "from you, May, I did not expect reproaches."

"They are not reproaches, Claude. Witness these tears, that I speak in all the sadness of grief, and not in anger. Hark! Do you understand those shouts?"

"I do not."

"The mob congratulates itself upon the escape of a criminal, and even I am from this moment involved in your guilt and your shame. I who by word or deed have wronged no one, am at last betrayed, even by my better feelings, to be the partner of iniquity. Your guilt is now my guilt, for I have received and continue to shelter the guilty man, against whom the hand of justice is raised. Thus Claude, no man can err, but he brings sin and sorrow upon others as well as himself."

"This state of things can soon be altered," said Claude, bitterly. "The window by which you but a few moments since admitted me, is close at hand. I will relieve you from the weight of my presence by leaving this house in the manner that I entered it, and the first declaration I make to my captors, shall be one exculpatory of you, for I will declare that instead of affording an asylum to the highwayman, you, with the bitterest reproaches, refused him one. Farewell."

"Claude, Claude."

He waved his hand, and strode into the dark room.

With a cry of dismay May rushed after him, and while his hand was upon the shutters, flung herself into his arms.

"Claude. Brother. Take my heart from my bosom and see how yet you dwell in its inmost recesses. Oh, Claude—Claude, if I could but die for you!"

"Let me go, May, I know I am unworthy of your affection. I know you did all you could to turn me from the course of life I have adopted, but I would not take your counsel, and therefore it is unfair of me now to involve you in any difficulty for my sake. I am lost, I know, and the steps in life that I have taken I cannot recede from. I do not now speak in anger, May."

"No—no, Claude. You shall not go."

"Nay, I pray you let me. It was the thoughtlessness of a moment that made me accept an asylum here. When I saw you on the balcony—of all houses in this great city, I ought to have avoided this."

May clung to him still, and he could not without absolute violence have extricated himself from her embrace, and that, of course, he was loth to use, so that she succeeded in detaining him until the procession of the doomed man, and the roar of the multitude of people that accompanied it were past, and but a confused murmur came upon their ears.

Claude listened attentively, and then turning to May, he said:

"Sister, it is rather sad to meet thus. How have you fared since last we parted? I have thought of you day and night, and sought you, and employed others to seek you, but all in vain. My eyes never rested upon your face until I stopped the coach on Ealing Common, in which, to my surprise, I found you seated. I nearly fell from my horse in the suddenness of the recognition. I knew your voice, and yet could scarce believe it was you. I thought some resemblance of tones might have cheated me, but when I came to look at the little bead purse you handed to me, and knew it had been our mother's, I could no longer doubt."

"Yes, Claude, it was our mother's, and it is the only relic I have of her—I thought it might arouse dormant feelings within your breast, and make virtue once more an inmate of your heart. Did you not feel something, when you looked upon it?"

"There is a gulf, May, now between me and innocence, that I may never hope to pass. You got back that purse with my tears and kisses upon it."

"Oh, Claude, you are not lost."

"You know not what you say."

"Yes, Claude. Indeed, indeed I do. There is—there always is, even in this life, a future for those who have the courage to dedicate it to virtue. Do not delude yourself with the vain and specious argument, that because you have sinned, you must still sin."

"But, May, would you have me, from some romantic notion of repentance, voluntarily give myself up to the hangman?"

"No, no, no—I—oh, no. That would not follow. Your better nature would so show itself, that for once an attribute of Heaven—mercy—would be borrowed by those who hold the scales of human justice, and you would be spared."

"Alas! my May, you speak more, much more like the heroine of some romance, than as one who, in this matter-of-fact world, has known what sorrow is. I tell you, sister, that having chosen, and so far proceeded in my present course of life, I have no hope, no chance of any other. I must now, like the forlorn hope of an army, push on, as the only chance of preserving, for yet awhile, my existence."

The sound of carriage wheels suddenly pausing in the street below now attracted the attention of both brother and sister, and May trembled, as she said:

"It is Mrs. Brereton, and—and——"

"She whom I heard named Cicely," exclaimed Claude. "I bless the danger that has taught me there is once more a chance of gazing on that lovely face."

"Are you mad, Claude? What can you mean? If they should find you here, what can I say? I am lost—lost!"

"How, sister? I am not ugly enough to frighten them, am I?"

"Can you jest at such a time as this? Oh, Claude, what shall I do? When I was friendless and destitute in the streets of London, chance, or the goodness of Heaven, brought me in contact with these ladies. I told them that I had no home, but I concealed my real name, and called myself May Russel. Since then they have afforded me an asylum. Oh, if they should now find they had been deceived, and that I was sister to a—a——"

"Highwayman, you would say."

A sharp rat-tat at the street door interrupted the conversation, and May glanced about her in a distracted manner.

"You must hide, Claude," she said; "you must hide."

"Wherever you please," he replied. "Only place me somewhere where I shall have a chance of seeing the young lady, named Cicely, that is all I ask, and I shall be patient, if I am forced to remain twelve months, wherever you place me."

There was a large cupboard in the room, close to the fireplace, and into that May hastily pushed Claude, and shut the door upon him, just as the street door closed again, after admitting the ladies Brereton to the house, and May had only just time to open the shutters of the front room before they ascended the stairs.

CHAPTER XII.

A SURPRISE—CLAUDE'S ESCAPE—A DRIVE TO
NEWGATE—THE ROAD AGAIN.

IT is true that a servant-girl, who was in the kitchen of the house at the time Claude Duval had taken refuge in it, might have been cognizant of the fact, but when the riot began, and the whole street was in an uproar, she had prudently got into the coal-cellar, nor did she emerge therefrom until the ladies Brereton—who, upon their arrival in London, had taken for a short time that house, furnished as it was—knocked at the door.

Thus it was that not only was Claude's presence unknown to the ladies, but May had had the opportunity of holding the brief and agitated conversation with him which we have recorded, and which, as is usual enough with

such arguments, convinced neither party, while it certainly had the effect of paining both.

"Oh, mum," said the girl to Miss Brereton, "there's been such a *riotation* in the streets, mum. They have been taking Thirty-two-string Jack to be hung, mum—leastways, I ain't quite sure that's the number of strings, but it's something like that, mum."

"How alarmed you look, Ann," said Cicely.

"Yes, miss, I is all that. Will you walk up? There's a good fire in the drawing-room. Oh, you would have been *scarified*, if you had been here, miss, when the *riotation* was. I got in the cellar, and so heard it all over my own head, though I couldn't see much of it, in consequence, you see, miss, of the roof."

Cicely was evidently in a dejected state, but, as she ascended the staircase, the peculiar phraseology of Ann extorted even a smile from her.

May was in hopes that the ladies would go into the front room; but, to her chagrin—for she was not very mindful of Claude's request, that he might be placed somewhere where he could command a view of Cicely—they sat down in the back room, and old Mrs. Brereton, after a few remarks, looked closely at May, and said:

"Why, child you have been crying."

"Have I, madam?" said May, scarcely knowing, in her confusion, what she replied to the most inopportune, but yet kind, inquiry.

"Your eyes tell that you have. Look at her, Cicely. Ah, my dear! what have you to cry for? You are not, as I am, full of grief and uncertainty regarding a son."

"Or as I am regarding a brother," said Cicely.

May could hardly restrain her tears from flowing afresh at this, but by a great effort she put on a show of outward composure, as she said:

"Then all inquiry regarding Mr. Markham Brereton is fruitless?"

"Quite so," said Cicely. "It is clear that my brother has not arrived in London, or he would have gone to Mr. Hammerston, the lawyer, to ascertain where we were staying. How strange it is that we should hear nothing of him since he trotted on to see that the road was clear as we came to town. Do you recollect, May? I do not, but my mother thinks the highwayman who stopped the carriage said something to intimate that he had met Markham."

"He did," said May, in a half-stifled tone.

"But what was it, my dear?" said the old lady.

"It was only an intimation that he had been informed that there was an invalid in the carriage, and who else but Mr. Brereton could so have informed him?"

"But Markham is reticent to strangers, rather than communicative," said Cicely.

"Certainly he is," added Mrs. Brereton. "Alas—alas! all these things will bring me to my grave; I can see that."

The old lady's tears began to flow, and May

blamed herself for not asking explicitly of Claude if he had had any encounter with Mr. Mark Brereton.

There was a painful silence of a few moments duration, which was interrupted by a slight exclamation from Cicely, who picked up from the floor, close to her feet, a small piece of folded paper.

"What is it?" cried May.

"I know not," replied Cicely. "It seemed to fall at my feet only just now."

She opened the paper, and, to the surprise of herself and her mother, read the following words:

"Mr. Brereton did meet Claude Duval, but he is not hurt, and will soon be with you."

"Gracious Heavens!" cried Mrs. Brereton, "who wrote that?"

"Are we in a land of enchantment?" cried Cicely.

May trembled, for well she knew that her brother had projected the little billet through a rather wide gap at the top of the cupboard door, but she spoke hastily, to avert, if possible, anything in the shape of further inquiry or speculation, saying:

"Perhaps someone in the street entangled it in your dress."

"It must have been so," replied Cicely. "Indeed, it cannot be accounted for in any other way. Mother, shall we believe it, and take comfort from it?"

At this moment there was heard a hurried footstep upon the stairs.

The door was flung open, and Markham Brereton rushed into his mother's arms. He was rather pale, and had a slight cut across one of his brows, but otherwise he looked well enough, and was evidently not seriously injured.

After the first joyful burst of congratulation upon his arrival had subsided, he spoke of his adventures on the road.

"I've just come from Mr. Hammerston," he said, "in Lincoln's Inn, and he told me that you had not left his chambers a quarter-of-an-hour. But you will be anxious to know what became of me when I started on in advance of the carriage."

"Oh, yes, yes," said Cicely. "Tell us all."

"Well, I was stopped by a highwayman, and got the worst of a little tussle, I suppose, for, after it was all over, I found myself in a labourer's cottage, he having found me lying stunned on the common. It's a wonder it was no worse, for I fired a shot at the fellow."

"Which he did not return?" said May.

"No! He behaved, as far as that goes, generously enough; but Mr. Hammerston tells me an odd tale of your adventures, and says that Tom Brereton, our most unwelcome cousin, has unaccountably disappeared."

"So it would seem," replied Cicely; "and Mr. Hammerston says that if he does not appear, with the legal documents he has in his pocket-book, that he will not be able to take the estate from us, as we have possession, but——"

"Nay, sister, it is his.'

"I was going to say so, Markham, when you interrupted me, and we said as much to Mr. Hammerston, who replied, that at all events, if we were so just, Mr. Tom could be forced to be a little generous, and not harass us about what we have already had and expended, under the impression that it was all our own."

"True, and I think that so far, we have a right to take advantage of circumstances. However, he may make his appearance again after all, with his papers."

"I am sure," said Mrs. Brereton, "that the highwayman took his pocket-book."

"Ah!" said Markham, "and the contents, most likely, are by this time in the fire. By-the-by, there are several men hanging about this house, and, as I came in, they looked very hard at me indeed, as if I had some sinister purpose in view. What can it mean?"

May was ready to drop from agitation, which was, however, luckily for her, not observed, and Markham went to the window to look out, to see if the men were still watching the house, little suspecting that they were officers, who had the best possible reason for supposing Claude Duval to be concealed on the premises.

Their intention was to wait until the return of their comrades from the execution of Sixteen-string Jack, and then to make an attack upon the house.

As he looked from the window, Markham, to his extreme surprise, saw a horseman coming down the road, whom he knew to be no other than Tom Brereton; but so bespattered with mud and dirt was he, that scarcely a vestige of his clothing was left free. His face, too, was horribly scratched, and a more deplorable figure than, on the whole, he presented, could not have been imagined.

"Here's an apparition!" cried Markham.

Cicely and her mother, as well as May, ran to the window, and there, sure enough, they saw the victimized Tom, and, on the impulse of the moment, Markham threw open the window, and called aloud to him:

"Good Heavens! is that you, Tom Brereton?"

At the voice, Tom looked up, uttered a hideous groan, and relaxing his hold of the horse, rolled off it, close to the threshold of the house.

Cicely looked all amazement, and Markham ran downstairs to the street door, to know what on earth could have reduced Tom to so miserable a plight, for his feelings towards him were much more those of contempt than anything else, while none of the family was so unjust as to blame him for claiming what was his own. The only objection they urged to his proceeding was, that he made his claim roughly, and carried it beyond their means of restoration.

"Why, what's the matter?" cried Markham, when he had dragged Tom into the passage.

"Oh! oh! oh!"

"Well, you can say something besides 'oh!' I suppose?"

"No, I can't."

"Why, you are covered with mud. Have you been riding a steeplechase?"

"I don't know, but I daresay I have as I came along. Oh, dear! oh, dear! They soon caught me, and wasn't I thankful; then they upset me, and wasn't I glad; then they collared me, after rolling me in the mud, and then, what do you think?"

"I really don't know what to think."

"They said I was Claude Duval, the great highwayman."

"You Claude Duval?"

"Yes, to be sure; that's why they ran after me, crying, 'Stop him!' Ah, I have had such a job! They soon found out I wasn't the highwayman, however; but I'll tell you all about it soon. Only let me lie down, somewhere, for a little while, and get off these horrid muddy clothes."

"I don't know, cousin Tom," said Markham, "that we are particularly called upon to show you any courtesy, for you were rather scant of that article with us, but it is not my disposition to return evil for evil, and as this is for the time being our home, you can come in, and I will see that you are accommodated with a bed."

"Oh, thank you. You haven't seen anything of my black pocket-book, have you?"

"How should I know anything of it?"

"Ah, well! dear me. All my bones ache, they do indeed. Oh, oh, oh! Stop him— stop him. There goes the horse! Well, I thought at least I should keep that as a set-off against what I had lost; but I am certainly the most unlucky fellow. Oh dear!"

Markham assisted him upstairs to a bedroom, where he left him, to get rid, by himself, of some of the dirty apparel in which he was enveloped, before he questioned him any further regarding the manner in which he came to be so situated.

May, who had been most anxiously revolving the best means of getting the party out of the room in which Claude was concealed, had ordered Ann to lay lunch in the dining-room. It was now announced, and they all descended to it, May promising to join them immediately, but her object was to speak to Claude; so the moment the room was clear, she opened the cupboard, and, with a face as pale as death itself, confronted him.

"Fly—oh, fly," she said. "Fly at once, or all will be discovered, and, after the deceit I have practised, I can hope for no further friendship from those who have been so kind to me."

"Fear nothing, May, I may yet be able to protect you."

"It is not the loss of their protection, but the loss of their good opinion, that would cut me to the very heart."

"Nay, you will not lose the good opinion of anyone whose good opinion is worth the having; but I know this is no place for me."

"Then fly from it at once."

"Into the arms of the officers, do you mean? Did you not hear Mr. Brereton say that men were watching the house? For whom do they watch, but for Claude Duval?"

"Alas! alas! What can be done?"

"I scarcely know, yet. But while I am thinking about it, take this pocket-book. It did belong to the young man called Tom, who was in the carriage with you all. It contains various documents connected with his property as well as the proofs of his personal identity. I wish you to give it to Mr. Brereton."

"How am I to do that, Claude?"

"Place it somewhere in such a position that he cannot fail to see it, and now tell me, is there any possibility of getting on the top of the house?"

"Yes, I think there is."

"Then do you go down to your lunch, and leave me to manage my own escape. What's that noise and shouting in the street?"

May ran to the window, and looked.

"It is the cavalcade returning from the execution of Sixteen-string Jack," she said.

"Ah, poor Jack!" said Claude. "Well, well, that's past now."

"Claude, Claude, they stop here. The officers dismount. They advance to the house. Oh, Claude—you are lost—lost!"

"All are not lost who are in danger, May. Go downstairs, and whatever may happen express no surprise or apprehension. Even if you should see me taken, I charge you, by the affection I know you still bear to me, to say nothing."

He dashed up the staircase, as he spoke, towards the bedrooms of the house, and as he did so he heard a clamorous knocking at the door.

Now, Claude had had not the most distant idea that Tom Brereton had been brought into the house, and when he went hurriedly into the first room he came to in order to see what its capabilities of concealment were, he was not a little surprised to find a man in bed, looking the picture of fright.

"Murder, murder!" said Tom; "what's that?"

"Why, who are you?" said Claude.

They confronted each other for a few moments in silence, the thoughts of each being busy in very different ways.

Claude was considering how he could turn this meeting to his advantage in the way of his escape, and Tom was wondering to see by his bedside a man in quaker garments, with anything but the manner and countenance of a quaker.

"Oh, dear, who are you?" added Tom.

"Are you the fellow that was robbed by Claude Duval," said Claude, "and made to gallop away upon a horse, with six men after you?"

"Yes—oh, dear, yes!"

"Then your life is not worth two minutes' purchase. I would not give a farthing for it, for you will be a dead man in five minutes!"

CHAPTER XIII.

THE SECOND ADVENTURE OF TOM BRERETON— CLAUDE'S ESCAPE.

WHEN Claude Duval uttered these words to the terrified and already nearly distracted Tom Brereton, the latter glared at him with such a comical expression of face, that if he, Claude, had not been seriously bent upon mischief, he must have laughed.

As it was, however, he contrived to keep something like a grave countenance, as he repeated:

"Yes, you are even now, in fact, a dead man!"

"A—dead—man? Oh, oh! Mur——"

"Hush! Such exclamations can only hasten a catastrophe which I would willingly prevent, if possible. Listen to me. It will be some satisfaction to you to know, in your last moments, why it is you are sacrificed. Listen."

Tom only glared at Claude with a bewildered look, and trembled so that he shook the whole bed, and set the rings by which the hangings were suspended jingling furiously.

"You are aware," added Claude, "that you were robbed by that celebrated highwayman, Claude Duval, who took away your black pocket-book, and who afterwards, to avert pursuit from himself, got you mounted on a horse, and set you off at a full gallop, with half-a-dozen men after you, who thought they were pursuing him."

"Oh, yes—yes!"

"Well, Claude has been taken, and it is believed by all the highwaymen and cracksmen in London that you were at the bottom of a deep-laid scheme for his capture, and have, in fact, been successful in effecting it, the consequence of which is that, dreading your power and *finesse*, they have come to the determination to destroy you."

"But it isn't true. I have got no power— no *finesse*. Oh, dear, oh, dear!"

"That's likely enough; but you won't make them believe it."

"Then what am I to do? Who are you?"

"I am the chief of the Bow Street runners, and will save you if I can; only you must obey me implicitly."

"I will, I will. Hark! do you hear that?"

"Yes, they have forced open the street-door."

While he was speaking to Tom Brereton, Claude had cast his eyes anxiously about the room, and in one corner he had espied a large chest, to which he now pointed, saying: •

"I suppose you have no particular objection to get in there?"

"In where?"

"In that chest. It strikes me that by so doing you may save yourself; I can just at present see no other way of aiding you. The thieves who are looking for you, expressly to take vengeance upon you, will probably not think of looking in there, while I, with some of my fellow officers, will come and take the chest away to a place of safety with you in it."

"Well, but——"

"As you please, your fate be upon your own head. All I have to do is to go and make oath before the magistrate at Bow Street, that I offered you a mode of escape which you thought proper to reject. I have the honour of bidding you good-day, sir."

"Oh, no, no. Stop, I—I will do it. Oh, dear, what a sad thing it is to be so knocked about, to be sure. I have only just escaped from the back of a wild horse, and now I am forced to get into a great box."

"It is the fortune of war."

"Is it? But I don't want to be at war with anybody; I only want to be quiet, that's all. The idea now of anybody thinking that I laid a deep scheme for anybody. I wish I could lay one to get home again, and be in peace and comfort, that I do. I know all this will be the death of me."

With groans and sighs, Tom got out of bed, and having hastily dressed himself, with no little difficulty got into the chest, which, as the key was in the lock, Claude securely fastened; and then, just as he heard the sound of footsteps on the stairs, he darted into the bed, and covered up all but his face with the abundant clothing that was on it.

The door of the room was dashed open in another moment, and eight or ten officers entered. They were well armed, for they evidently expected some resistance, in the capture of such a man as Claude Duval.

They looked rather disappointed, when they only found a bedroom and a man lying in bed, with a languid aspect, which Claude put on very consistently.

"Oh, gentlemen, gentlemen!" he said. "Who are you? Oh! tell me who you are?"

"Who are you?" cried one of the officers.

"I hardly know, for I can't exactly say whether I'm asleep or awake, gentlemen. I was asleep, but—that is to say, I think I was asleep, and then my name was Mr. Brereton, but just now a fellow came bang into the room with a pistol in his hand."

"A pistol. That must be our man. Was it Claude Duval?"

"Who?"

"Claude Duval, the great highwayman."

"How should I know? I'm a respectable man, and have no such acquaintance."

"Where did he go?"

"I was telling you, but you are so impatient. He held the pistol against my head, and, says he, 'say one word and you are a dead man,' says he, 'for may my mare 'Nell' lose her wind, if I don't blow your brains out.'"

"It's our man!" cried the officers. "There can be no mistake now; where did he go?"

"Well, I'm a-telling you, but you get so furious. You must be a sad fellow at home, that you must—my father was a woolstapler, and he often used to say to me, 'Tom,' said he, 'whenever you——'"

"Confound your father! We want to know where Claude Duval went."

"Well, I'm a-telling you. He didn't wait for me to say anything, but after he had threatened my life in a manner of speaking, he popped into that great box there."

The officers raised a shout of exultation, and three or four of them rushed towards the chest, and sat down on the lid.

"Ha! ha! ha!" laughed he who had carried on the brief conversation with Claude. "Ha! ha! ha! I rather think we have the fox in a trap now."

"Oh, you needn't be afraid of his getting out," said Claude; "I forgot to tell you that he asked me to lock it up, and take the key, and say my clothes were in it, that's all, and I did lock it, and here's the key, gentlemen."

There was at this moment some half-stifled cry from the box, but it was not sufficiently clear to be understood, and the officers felt then that assurance was doubly sure.

"What say you, comrades?" said one. "We know that our prisoner is a troublesome fellow, suppose we take him off to Newgate just as he is, box and all?"

"That's an uncommonly good idea," said Claude.

"So it is," said the others, for they all seemed to shrink from a personal encounter with so redoubtable a personage as Claude Duval, and the opportunity of taking him away safely in a chest they considered was by no means to be slighted.

A furious knocking arose from the inside of the box, which convinced Claude that Tom Brereton had heard sufficient of the conversation to find out how he had been imposed upon, but the officers would by no means consent to his release, and the more violently he kicked the panels of the chest, the more intent were they upon getting him away just as he was.

"We are very much obliged to you, sir," said the principal of them to Claude. "Very much obliged, indeed, so now we will take away your troublesome customer, and you may be quite sure you will never be troubled with him any more, for he will be hanged at Tyburn next sessions, as safe as we have him here in the box."

"No doubt of that," said Claude. "I'd take my oath of it, I would, gentlemen, and when he is hanged, you may take your oaths I shall be there, and in the best place, too."

The officers took up the chest among them, and staggered down the stairs with it, while one preceded the others, and called loudly for a cart in which to carry the treasure to Newgate.

One was soon pressed into the service, and away the whole party went, most specially delighted with the success that had crowned their efforts, and quite congratulating themselves that there were no more of them to share the £200 reward amongst.

"Well, Mr. Tom Brereton," soliloquized Claude, as he sprang from the bed, when the officers had fairly departed, "you are doomed

to be of great service to me. Twice have I owed my escape to your accidentally coming into my way, but the mistake will be discovered as soon as they get to Newgate, and, perhaps, sooner, so this is no place for me."

He stood at the door and listened for a few moments, and then, not hearing anyone stirring in the lower part of the house, he cautiously slipped downstairs, and reached the passage in perfect safety.

Just, however, as he was passing the dining-room door, he heard the sounds of weeping in the room, and peeping through the crevice of the door, he saw Cicely Brereton sitting at a table, absorbed in grief.

"My poor, dear mother," she said; "she is at last no more. Alas, alas, when will Mark return with the physicians?"

"What can be the meaning of this?" thought Claude. "Why, the old lady must have died suddenly. How beautiful Cicely is, and yet how absurd it is of me to continue thus looking at her, and drinking in such deep draughts of love. She can never be more to me than a beautiful picture. Oh, would that I had never seen her, for then I should have continued to be the same careless fellow I was, but which now I can never be again, for the thought will at times come over me, that by a different course of life, I might almost have made myself worthy of such a treasure as Cicely Brereton."

He felt that he ought to go at once, and yet, while there was still the opportunity of looking at the beautiful girl, he could not make up his mind to tear himself away, but, like a worshipper at some shrine, stood in an attitude of rapt devotion.

Suddenly she rose, and approached the door.

He had not time to leave the passage, and in another moment they were face to face.

A slight scream came from the lips of Cicely.

"Be not alarmed," said Claude; "you never in all your life, Cicely Brereton, had less cause for fear."

"Who, and what are you?"

"Pardon me, if I reply to neither question, and likewise pardon me for saying, that although there is not, and cannot be, the most distant shadow of a hope in my mind of ever calling you mine, yet I love you as never yet man loved, for it is a love without hope, and yet complete."

Without giving her time to make any reply to this most singular declaration of attachment, he took her hand, and for one moment pressed it to his lips.

In the next he was gone, and May (who had been in the back room, with the corpse of old Mrs. Brereton, who had suddenly expired without a sigh), hearing voices, made her appearance in time to see the street-door shut after him. She did not, however, see that it was her brother Claude.

"Oh, May—May!" said Cicely. "Who has been here?"

"I know not."

"A man in gray clothing, and—and handsome, yet bold. There was something, too, in the tones of his voice that I seemed to remember. He has just left the house."

"Thank Heaven!" exclaimed May, for she knew that he was in safety, although how he had managed to effect his escape from the officers, she could not tell.

"Yes, thank Heaven!" said Cicely.

"Yes—yes! At such a time as this surely we want no visitors, Cicely. Oh, that Markham would return!"

Markham did return quickly, bringing with him the nearest physician; but all the skill and all the learning that the world ever saw could not again have rekindled the flame of existence in the now senseless form of Mrs. Brereton.

CHAPTER XIV.

THE SPY—A LAST RIDE—THE "REINDEER" AT MOORFIELDS.

CLAUDE, when he reached the street, looked neither to the right nor to the left. In the first place he felt confident that all the officers had departed with Tom Brereton and the box to Newgate, and, even if he were wrong, and anyone had lingered on the spot, his looking for him would not make the danger of an encounter with him the less; so Claude walked on with as measured an appearance as any chance passenger could wish to have.

"I would give a good round sum," he murmured, "if I could only be present when the officers open the box, and discover how egregiously they have been duped. But that little gratification is not to be thought of, much as I should enjoy it. It was a bold stroke, and succeeded beyond my expectations."

But, despite these reflections, and his seemingly unconcerned manner, Claude's eyes and ears were open to catch the slightest movement. The atmosphere of continual danger in which he lived had sharpened his perceptive faculties to a remarkable extent.

He was just congratulating himself upon the fact that he was apparently unwatched, when he became conscious that a shabby-looking man was creeping after him.

In order to make sure that his imagination was not deceiving him, he turned suddenly and sharply, and walked a few paces in the contrary direction, when the shabby-looking man was so confounded by this unexpected manœuvre, that he ran into a doorway, which proceeding quite convinced Claude that he was right in his first conjecture, and that this man, for some object, was watching him.

This was not a state of things that he was likely to allow to continue, so he slackened his pace just as he arrived opposite to a stand of hackney-coaches, and turned again as abruptly as before.

Reaching the man before he could get out of the way, he said:

"What do you want with me?"

"I beg your pardon, sir," said the man.

"For what?"

"Why—a—a—I—you see I'm no fool—I know what I know."

"And what's that?"

"You are Claude Duval."

"Well?"

This answer of Claude's took the spy so much by surprise, that he could not tell for a moment or two how to reply to it; but then feeling that what he had to say must be said quickly, he strove to put on an appearance of boldness as he spoke.

"I am a police spy," he said. "The officers employ me to ferret out things, sir. They pay me badly. Give me a £20 note, and I don't see you at all till the next time. They think they have you, but I did not, so I lingered about the house, and you see I am right. Here you are, sir."

"And why don't you take me? You know there is a reward of £200 to whoever will lodge me in Newgate."

"Yes, sir; but then, I—I would rather not try to do such a thing—I'm afraid you would not let me. Ha! ha! You understand, sir."

"Perfectly. You are afraid."

"Well, I—I—you may call it so if you like, sir. Twenty pounds is not much for a gentleman like you, who gets your money so easy, you know."

"But if I have not got it?"

"Why, then, I'm afraid I shall have to stick by you, and call for help, and share the reward with some half-dozen people who may come to my assistance."

"Well, well," said Claude, with a smile. "You shall have what you so absolutely require of me. Call a coach, will you?"

The spy beckoned to a coachman, and a vehicle from the stand came to the curbstone. The driver, with all his greatcoats, let down the steps, and adjusted the straw in the inside, while Claude and the spy stood close to the large window of a confectioner's shop.

"Well, coachman," said Claude, "you see this gentleman by my side? He is what is called a bum-bailiff. Take a good look at him."

The coachman stared, and so did the spy, but they had neither of them time for much reflection, for Claude suddenly pounced upon the latter, and, seizing him by the back of the neck with one hand, and about the middle with the other, flung him through the confectioner's window with such tremendous force that he carried all before him.

There was a crash of glass, a yell from the spy, and a scream from the young lady in the shop, who had been reading a novel when she was thus intruded upon.

"My eye!" exclaimed the coachman.

"Drive round two turnings, and then put me down," cried Claude Duval, as he jumped into the coach. "You shall have a guinea for this job."

Never did the coachman spring upon his seat with more activity, never were the old

www.ingramcontent.com/pod-product-compliance
Lightning Source LLC
Chambersburg PA
CBHW082052220626
47052CB00006B/1218